PENGUIN BOOKS
NEVER GONE

One of the youngest published authors in the country, Anusha Subramanian was only twelve when she wrote her first book, *Heirs of Catriona*. Her hobbies include reading, binge watching television shows and writing, of course. Why wait for someone else to do it when you can write your own fairy tale, right?

You can connect with her on twitter @AnushaS_

never gone

Anusha Subramanian

PENGUIN BOOKS

An imprint of Penguin Random House

PENGUIN BOOKS

USA | Canada | UK | Ireland | Australia
New Zealand | India | South Africa | China | Singapore

Penguin Books is part of the Penguin Random House group of companies
whose addresses can be found at global.penguinrandomhouse.com

Published by Penguin Random House India Pvt. Ltd
4th Floor, Capital Tower 1, MG Road,
Gurugram 122 002, Haryana, India

First published in Penguin Books by Penguin Random House India 2016

ISBN 9780143424963

Typeset in Joanna MT by Manipal Digital Systems, Manipal
Printed at Repro India Limited

www.penguin.co.in

This is a legitimate digitally printed version of the book and therefore might not
have certain extra finishing on the cover.

To Kirtana Ananth and Kabir Walia,
two of the most important people in my life

Prologue

Ananya Krishnan relaxed at the sound of the bell.

Before all the students could even shut their books, she had grabbed her lunch box and dashed out of the classroom. Two seconds later she stood in front of XI C, scanning the crowd for familiar faces. Incessant chatter, the grating sounds of desks and chairs being rearranged, bags shifting, random shrieking and laughter assaulted her ears. Lunch breaks were a busy time for everyone, and after being 'well-behaved' for nearly three hours at a stretch, the students could barely sit still. A smile tugged at her lips when she finally spotted Veera—her best friend since Class IV—and made her way over to her, carefully navigating through the sea of students.

'Finally!' she exclaimed as she plonked her lunch box on the table and collapsed gratefully into the chair that might as well have been reserved for her. Lunch breaks at Agastya International School were half-an-hour long and the students made full use of its every second. Every year, the school shuffled its students arbitrarily into different sections because of which Ananya and her friends often found themselves separated. But at least they could blame the teachers for that. Now that they were in Class XI and had to decide what they wanted to study further, being in different sections was inevitable, and there was no one to blame it on. So these thirty minutes were all they got to be together.

'Help me!' Veera Vishwanathan groaned loudly. 'I *cannot* study any more. I'm dying! I hate being in the eleventh!'

Her jet-black hair was tied into a neat plait in accordance with school regulations and her almond-shaped eyes were thickly rimmed with kajal. Tan, tall and slim, she made the school uniform look like a model's outfit. It always surprised Ananya that Veera was so completely unaware of how beautiful she was. The best thing about Veera was just how unafraid she was to be herself. She was unabashed about what she liked and what she didn't. She wasn't swayed by trends or fads that saw a temporary burst of popularity. She was the kind of girl who preferred plain milk to coffee, dal chawal to pizza, and was insanely productive for someone who slept as much as she did.

'The terminals are barely over, and they're grilling us already,' Ananya grimaced. The hot Mumbai sun streamed in from the windows, making her skin look pale gold.

'No, no, we are NOT talking about depressing stuff today!' A ridiculously large steel lunch box crashed down on the desk, making Ananya and Veera jump. They didn't have to look up to see who it was.

Aslesha Narayan. To call her loud and crazy would be an understatement.

Veera rolled her eyes. 'Let's hear it . . . What's got you so excited?'

'Get ready to hear the biggest piece of news in the house.' Aslesha's voice turned overly dramatic. Neither Veera nor

Ananya batted an eyelid. This was routine behaviour. Aslesha aka Lame Jokes Queen aka Gossip Girl obsessed about everything to do with everyone. So this 'news' would be lame at worst, or entertaining at the very least.

'Niharika is going to ask Siddharth out!'

The statement hung in the air for a split second as they took it in.

Veera coughed violently while Ananya's jaw dropped open. This was serious news. Siddharth was their 'guy best friend' (as the term goes). And Niharika was one of those regular girls whose popularity had shot up because she had made friends with all the 'right' people.

Before either of them could splutter out a response, Kavya, her eyes ablaze with anger in a way they hadn't seen for quite some time, turned up at their desk. She was fuming.

'That Niharika is a BIT—'

'Volume!' Ananya shushed Kavya, quickly glancing around to see if Niharika or any of her friends had heard Kavya's outburst.

Kavya's face was flushed with anger. 'You know she's evil! And manipulative! And—'

'Okay, stop!' Aslesha held up her hands. She turned to Veera and Ananya. 'See? I know what I'm talking about!'

Kavya Dhar's reputation as a social butterfly demanded that she socialize with everyone else before joining her friends in XI C for lunch. She was the shortest of the four, but she made up for what she lacked in height with her stunning figure and gorgeous hair. She was tiny but fiery.

She was also Siddharth's ex.

3

While they were in a relationship, they were everyone's OTP because they had been together for one-and-a-half years in a school where the longest relationships lasted a week. But the people who knew them well never expected them to last, since they were always getting into fights, and their relationship was mostly 'textual'. They were too young, too awkward and too involved with other things to have a smooth relationship. Siddharth wanted complete commitment and Kavya wasn't comfortable with that. The way things turned out was no one's fault, but because Siddharth was the one to end it, Kavya got to take the moral high ground.

'So soon? We just broke up! How could he move on so fast?' Kavya whined. She pulled up a chair and sat down, opening her lunch box. 'Plus, how can a girl make the first move? That's so needy!'

'She is going to ask him, I said. Niharika hasn't asked him out yet,' Aslesha said. In a weird way, Aslesha and Kavya balanced each other out. Aslesha was the yin to Kavya's yang.

'And it's not like Siddharth is going to say yes!' Veera said confidently. 'I don't even think it's true.'

Kavya nodded thoughtfully, twirling her fork in her cold noodles.

'So are you saying you still like him, Kavya?' Ananya asked in what she hoped was an indifferent tone. She wasn't even sure why she'd asked that. It wasn't like it mattered any more.

Kavya's head snapped up. 'No, of course not. I'm just irritated that those one-and-a-half years of my life were worth nothing! Plus, I could have a hundred guys queue up for me if I wanted.'

Veera's mouth was a thin line as she held back her annoyance. What Kavya had said was true; most people in their school thought she was hot. But her self-obsession never failed to get on everyone's nerves. Veera wished she would let go of her I-couldn't-care-less act once in a while.

Kavya shut her lunch box. 'I'll see y'all in a while,' she said, and left the classroom. The rest of them knew her well enough to understand that she wasn't going to be back before the lunch break ended. She had more people to meet, more gossiping to do and more guys to flirt with. But that was Kavya and they had accepted her quirky routine in the five years of their friendship.

'It's so obvious that she still likes him,' Veera sighed.

'Who are we kidding here? It's her ego that's hurt, not her!' Ananya retorted. 'She's more pissed that Siddharth moved on before she did!'

'Whose ego are we talking about?' Siddharth Ahuja suddenly appeared in front of them, running his fingers through his tousled hair, making it stand up in all directions. Behind nerdy black glasses—the ones you wear when you're trying to look nerdy—were equally black eyes that always sparkled with an intriguing mixture of laughter and curiosity. His lips twitched as he acknowledged the girls with a nod.

'Kavya's,' Veera said. 'And apparently Niharika is—'

'MORE FOOD!' Siddharth pointed at Ananya's lunch as Aslesha stifled a laugh. Veera let out a sigh of exasperation.

'So, word is that Nihari—'

'You didn't leave any pizza for me!' Siddharth whined to Aslesha. He reached for Ananya's lunch.

'Siddharth—' The irritation in Veera's voice was evident.

'This is *good*!' He wolfed down the noodles.

'Siddharth!'

'Okay, okay, what?' He turned to Veera with an amused look.

'Niharika-is-going-to-ask-you-out,' Veera finished in a rush, in case Siddharth decided to interrupt her again.

'Is she now?' He was indifferent.

'SIDDHARTH!'

'It's not true!' He laughed. 'It's a stupid rumour!'

'Why did you break up with Kavya anyway?' Veera asked cautiously.

'She's annoying,' he said.

'That's not good enough.' Veera crossed her arms.

Contrary to his open, friendly nature, Siddharth had completely clammed up about his break-up. His friends wondered if even Kavya knew the reason. They had ended rather abruptly, and it had most certainly not been a clean break. After their break-up, Siddharth would only talk to Aslesha, Ananya and Veera when Kavya wasn't around.

'Tell me!' Veera pushed Siddharth playfully.

As Ananya listened to the ongoing argument, she smiled. Veera could coax him to talk like nobody else could.

'I know you'll tell me eventually, Siddharth. So I'm not even going to bother asking,' Aslesha said, miffed at being ignored. Ananya gritted her teeth. Aslesha always behaved like she knew Siddharth best.

'Enough!' Ananya said. 'Anyway, I was thinking, let's all go out this Saturday?'

'Can't, I'm playing football with a few people,' he said absent-mindedly.

Ananya and Veera exchanged a look. Siddharth was unavailable again.

'Stop that!' Siddharth said.

'Stop what?' asked Ananya.

'That weird "look" thing that you and Veera do! It's like you're having a private conversation!' he laughed.

'It's instinctive! Can't help it,' Ananya shrugged.

'Really?' He inched closer to the unsuspecting Veera. In a flash he grabbed at her hair, pulling the scrunchy off her neat plait and messing up her hair. Veera launched herself at Siddharth, twisting to try and get her scrunchy back.

Ananya watched all this, thoroughly amused. Siddharth *always* did that and Veera *always* fell for it.

As Veera made a grab for his right hand, his free hand shot out and held her wrist.

Ananya saw Veera instantly stiffen. If she hadn't known Veera so well, she wouldn't have noticed the way Veera's breath, almost imperceptibly, caught in her throat. But the next minute, Veera had spun out of Siddharth's grip and snatched the scrunchy out of his hand. When Ananya glanced at Siddharth, she saw the ghost of a half-smile etched on his face, suggesting that he had willingly surrendered the scrunchy to Veera.

Ananya inhaled deeply. The look on Veera's face when Siddharth had grabbed her hand . . . how could she not have seen it before?

Before Ananya's train of thoughts could chug its way to fantasy land, Veera collapsed on the chair beside her, retying her hair triumphantly.

'What?' Veera asked, and Ananya realized she'd been staring.

'Anyway,' Aslesha said, muscling her way back into the conversation. She had been ignored for some time now and that didn't sit well with her. 'You cannot date Niharika. I will kill you if you do. She's not your type.'

'Yeah, because you know his type so well,' Veera muttered under her breath, too soft for Aslesha to hear, but Siddharth grinned.

'I don't get why you guys don't like her,' Siddharth said, shovelling some more food in his mouth. That boy had food in his mouth 99 per cent of the time. And the other 1 per cent he spent hunting for food. 'She's friendly.'

The violent, fake coughing that followed was enough to shut Siddharth up.

'Sure, Niharika is friendly . . . if friendly is the new fake,' Veera said nonchalantly.

'OH SNAP!' Aslesha laughed loud enough to make their classmates turn. Siddharth threw up his hands in surrender as Ananya grinned widely.

'Put your hands up cuz Kanye is IN THE HOUSE!' a voice boomed, and all the students in XI C collectively groaned. A chain of loud, obnoxious words followed, which they had all come to recognize as the music that preceded a beat-drop or a rap.

The students parted to allow Nikhil Shetty to pass through. A newcomer would have taken in his cropped hair, wiry but short build and intelligent eyes, and got the impression that he was a quiet, calm kid. That newcomer would have been wrong.

He was a high-IQ, street-smart specimen, a walking-talking encyclopedia of random, useless facts, who swore by rap music. His life's ambition was to earn a living by singing insanely obscene raps out on the streets. And God forbid if anyone should ever start an argument with him or question his facts.

'Hey, hey, hey!' He grabbed a chair and sat down, nearly knocking Siddharth over in the process. 'Let me put your racing hearts to rest. The moment y'all have been waiting for has finally arrived!' He spread his hands dramatically.

'Not again,' Siddharth rolled his eyes.

'In three . . .' Veera muttered.

'Two . . .' Aslesha shut her ears.

'One,' Ananya groaned.

Nikhil launched into an obnoxious rap, the words tumbling from his mouth in a cascade that refused to stop. They waited impatiently for it to end. There was no way on earth anybody could make him stop once he'd started. He called it 'pouring out his pain', though nobody understood why pouring out his pain had to be so painful for everyone else.

Finally, unable to bear it any longer, Siddharth shook Nikhil violently. 'Wow, okay—that's enough! Don't rap us to death just yet!'

Nikhil stopped rapping with a smirk and started drumming a tune on the wooden desk, channelling his hyperactive energy in a different direction. Siddharth leaned back on the desk and studied Ananya.

'What? Dude, you're freaking me out,' Ananya said, raising one eyebrow quizzically.

'Not to kill the vibe or anything,' he started cautiously, as though afraid that Ananya would bite, 'but I have news.'

'About what?' asked Ananya, unconcerned.

'About Aakash.'

The temperature in the room suddenly seemed to have dropped by ten degrees. Ananya sat up straight in her chair. Veera tensed as the strain in Ananya's posture seeped into her. Nikhil wet his lips, his fingers faltering on the wood.

'Forget it,' Ananya said clearly, her voice freezing.

'It's important.' Siddharth was insistent.

'I don't care how important it is,' Ananya said, enunciating every word clearly. 'How many times have I told you that I don't want to know anything about him, unless he tells me himself!'

Everyone gulped, but Siddharth pushed on, undaunted.

'Ananya, come on. Stop acting stupid about this,' he said, as Veera glared daggers at him, trying to make him handle this more tactfully. 'I don't understand what the big deal is!'

'You don't understand because there is nothing to understand!' Ananya's voice was remarkably stable. 'What I don't get is why you always bring me news about him and his life but never tell him anything about mine.'

'Listen, I'm just the messenger, don't shoot me!' Siddharth said, instantly defensive.

Veera laid a restraining hand on Ananya's arm. The facade of indifference that Ananya had so carefully built up over the past year couldn't be taken down now. But at the same time Veera wanted to know what Siddharth had to say.

'Hear him out, ya,' Veera whispered. When Ananya didn't say anything, she motioned for Siddharth to continue. Aakash and Siddharth were best friends, after all, and that made Siddharth a valuable source of information.

'There are rumours about him and this other girl,' he started carefully. 'Nothing concrete . . . just rumours . . . but I thought you should know.'

'Oh, yeah! I can't believe you didn't know. Siddharth told me that loooooong back!' Aslesha piped up, happy at last to hear her own voice.

'I wonder why you still tell her things, Siddharth,' Ananya said, not looking at Aslesha. 'Since she doesn't know when to open her mouth and when to keep it shut.'

Aslesha winced, shame wiping the smugness right off her face. Ananya still hadn't forgiven her for what had happened that night—Aslesha had crossed a line and her friendship with Ananya had shattered then. They used to be so close . . . but now, all she could detect was a sort of strange aloofness in Ananya's attitude towards her; she was never outright mean or angry, but the warmth between them was gone.

'Wait, am I missing something here?' Siddharth asked, looking from Ananya to Aslesha.

'Nothing,' Ananya said. She sighed, her shoulders relaxing. 'Sorry, Siddharth, I didn't mean to be rude to you. It's just that I try so hard to go back to how things were before . . . but it's like he doesn't even want to see my face.'

'*Ooookaaay.*' Nikhil hauled himself out of the chair. 'I'm outta here before this gets any filmier.'

Ananya managed a rueful smile. The bell trilled, signalling the end of their thirty minutes together. Ananya grabbed her lunch box and, smiling briefly at Veera, Siddharth and Aslesha, walked out.

Veera's heart ached to see Ananya like this. Break-ups were always bad, but this . . . this was another level. And referring to what happened between Ananya and Aakash as a 'break-up' seemed much too trivial and insulting. In fact, nothing about their relationship could be labelled. They protected each other like siblings, acted like best friends and never hesitated to rag each other. It was so easy yet so intense. They flouted the 'rules' of a 'relationship' (if you can call what they had one) and made their own. And now that Aakash wasn't with her, she constantly second-guessed herself, ignored her instincts and oscillated through a spectrum of feelings. It was exhausting her, and Veera could see it. What made it worse was that Ananya had to pretend she didn't care because Aakash seemed to be doing great on his own.

Ananya hurried out of the classroom, clutching her lunch box so tight that her knuckles had turned white. She needed some air; the heavy silence and the concerned looks were stifling. She raced up the stairs to the fourth floor.

Agastya International's main building had a central courtyard with the corridor running around it. It was always sunny in the corridors but right now, sunny was the last thing she was feeling.

Ananya saw groups of students still leaning over the parapet, talking to their friends and trading gossip hurriedly before the teacher walked into class.

Class wasn't even on her mind right now. She rushed towards a relatively empty section of the corridor and hurled herself on the parapet. Pressing her forehead to the cool marble-top, she let her thoughts drift.

Aakash Acharya. She hated him. Yeah right, who was she kidding? She liked him more than he could ever imagine. But it was much less painful to pretend that he didn't matter. They had been best friends once upon a time. Now she hated thinking about him. And she hated that she couldn't stop thinking about him.

When they did meet, Ananya and Aakash were perfectly civil to each other. But the underlying awkwardness that had seeped into their friendship was ever-present.

He had that cute, sort-of-geeky charm. But it was the intelligence in his eyes that she really loved. And the way she felt like she just belonged whenever he was around.

Even thinking about him now overwhelmed her. It would be so much easier to hate him if he were a jerk.

She took a deep breath and lifted her head. There were some things she couldn't change. Besides, she had everything she wanted in life—good grades, intelligence, amazing friends and no dearth of social activities. She even looked pretty good, except she was always conscious about her body; she wasn't fat but she wasn't skinny either. That wasn't such a big deal, though. She decided to be grateful for what a brilliant life she had, instead of cribbing over the one thing she didn't have.

But what if that was the most important of all things . . . she grumbled to herself as she walked, her head bent, towards her class.

Bone-rattling pain suddenly stabbed her shoulder and she realized as she looked up, wincing, that she had banged into someone.

'Oh, I'm sor—' The apology died on her lips as she saw whom she'd bumped into.

He nodded his head once in acknowledgement and then continued on his way. Suddenly feeling light-headed, Ananya steadied herself against the wall, staring at the retreating form of Mahir Shah.

Mahir Shah was the coolest boy at Agastya International. Tall and immensely good-looking, with perpetually windswept hair and tanned skin, he was the most popular guy in all of the eleventh, not to mention the hottest. He looked good and he knew it. A lot of people had taken a fancy to his I-don't-give-a-shit attitude and casual overconfidence. It hadn't taken him long to become the school's most popular boy. Ananya scrunched up her nose in distaste. Of course, he was part of the 'it' crowd, friends with all the fakest people she just couldn't stand, and never let go of an opportunity to show that off. He was a player, a colossal liar, a terrible attention-seeker and an accomplished flirt.

But Ananya also knew there was another side to him. The insecure, self-blaming, low-self-esteemed, heartbroken side. The part of him that he would do anything to keep hidden from the rest of the world.

She grimaced as the memories came flooding back. Uncountable hours spent on the phone trying to make him feel better, texting non-stop every day, stolen glances and his nods of acknowledgement . . . all of these details had lodged themselves firmly in a corner of her brain that flashed 'WARNING! He's not good for you'.

Veera always said that Mahir was using her whenever he needed someone. That just because Ananya had a soft spot for him didn't mean that he had one for her. But Ananya had a policy that she would trust everyone unless they gave her reason not to.

She shook her head. Thinking about Mahir and her relationship with him just left her feeling more muddled than ever.

Her eyes caught a flash of coloured fabric in a sea of white uniforms and she started.

'Shit!' she muttered as she saw her biology teacher round the corner. The bell had rung ages ago and she didn't want to get shouted at for going late to class. She raced down the corridor, mumbling apologies to several people as she elbowed them in her rush.

She burst into class, seconds before the teacher appeared at the door. Flashing a triumphant smile at her classmates, she collapsed into her chair gratefully.

'Let's go ahead with Vegetative Propagation.'

Ananya stole a glance at the clock. It was 1.45 p.m.—the period had only just started. There were two hours of school still left and that meant four study periods that she needed to sit—or actually, sleep—through. She glanced around at the other students who had already started taking notes. Digging out a refill pad from her bag, she settled into her seat and uncapped her pen, the teacher's monotonous voice already making her eyelids heavy.

It was going to be a long day.

Veera

Aneurysm.

Veera typed the letters on Google, her fingers shaking, the phone trembling in her hands.

Her lungs refused to take in air but her heart continued to pound furiously. Despite all this, she didn't *feel* anything. She understood. She registered. But she could form no attachment with whatever she'd been told.

She was like a spectator, watching her life play out from afar.

The call had come at 2 a.m. Before she knew it, her mom was shaking her awake, tears streaming down her face. Veera had bolted out of bed.

'Dad?' she whispered. Had something happened to her dad? Her mom shook her head, still unable to form a coherent sentence.

'Arjun?' she asked about her brother. '*Paati?*' Her voice rose with desperation as she thought of her grandmom.

Her mom collapsed on the bed.

'Ananya.'

Veera's heart stopped. Ananya? What could possibly have happened to Ananya? Was she changing schools? Or worse, had she got a transfer? But it was two in the freaking morning!

'MOM!' Veera shook her. 'What happened?'

Her mom whispered something.

'What? Mom, hold it together!'

'She's dead.'

'MOM!' Veera yelled. 'What are you saying?'

'I'm not joking, Veera,' her mom backtracked hurriedly, realizing that she had been brutal in her choice of words. 'It happened just a while ago . . . her mother just called.'

Time stopped for Veera. The walls of her room seemed to close in on her. Air. She needed air. Now. Pushing past her mother, she tried to make her way out of the room. She had to get away from here . . . anywhere but here.

But she had only taken a few steps when a wave of light-headedness swept over her. She didn't even try to regain her balance as her world tilted and she banged her head hard on the floor. The shock cleared her brain.

'Veera!' Her mom stumbled towards her. Veera felt like she was hearing her voice underwater. Everything seemed muted and hazy. All she could hear was a dull ringing in her ears. 'Are you okay?'

'Go. Just go.' Veera's voice trembled. She pressed her eyes shut until her head pounded. No! No . . . this couldn't be true. This was all a nightmare; she just had to wake up. *Dead, dead, dead* . . . The words echoed in her mind like a gruesome chant.

'Veera . . .?'

'LEAVE ME ALONE!'

Her mom left, shutting the door on her way out.

Veera curled into a ball. Her breathing was short and erratic. Dead? 'Death' was a tragedy that happened to *other* people. It couldn't possibly have happened to someone who was such an important presence in her life, could it?

Ananya was dead.

The words made no sense. She repeated it over and over in her head, trying to make sense of it—trying to *feel* something. None of this made sense. It wasn't true . . . it *couldn't* be true. She dug the heels of her palms into her eyelids harshly.

This was impossible.

She believed it with such conviction that, for a while, she had almost convinced herself. She didn't know how long she lay on her bedroom floor, curled up like a fetus, the cold from the marble seeping into her being. The ringing in her ears had barely subsided, and the will to do anything other than lie on the floor still evaded her.

She heard hushed voices outside her door. Her mom sniffing, the choked sobs of her brother, the heavy voice of her father and the hushed prayers of her paati.

Anger boiled up inside her. Didn't they understand that this was a lie? Ananya was healthy and alive!

The force of anger cleared her brain for a split second. It was nice to finally *feel* something, even if it was rage. She got up and opened the door. Immediately, the voices ceased. And she stood facing her entire family.

'Come on, Veera,' her mom said softly. 'We have to go to the hospital.'

'I'm not going anywhere.'

'Veera . . .' Her mom looked fragile. Arjun, Veera's dad and grandmom stood mutely beside her.

'There is absolutely no reason to go to the hospital at this unearthly hour because Ananya IS. NOT. DEAD. End of discussion.'

'They need our support! We need to be there for them!' her mom pressed on.

'You don't understand, Mom! SHE'S NOT DEAD!'

'Veera.' Her dad's arms encircled her.

'She. Is. Not. Dead! She's healthy and alive and probably asleep in her own bed in her own house, and not in some stupid hospital!' Veera said.

Her family exchanged pained glances but Veera rambled on.

'I spoke to her three hours ago! We have school tomorrow and I was supposed to meet her early so we could go up to the terrace. And we had dinner plans for tomorrow night, like we have every Friday, and we were supposed to finish our maths homework together. She was supposed to help me write my speech for the elocution competition, and we still have to get our dresses for the Christmas party in one month and . . .' Her voice cracked. 'She's not dead! She can't be . . .'

She would have collapsed if her father hadn't been holding her. 'She's not . . . she can't be!' Sobs racked her whole body and she convulsed violently. Frustration welled up like an angry snake. She felt the pain now, but the pain was detached—she still couldn't associate it with herself.

Even in the next fifteen minutes that it took for her to be bundled into the car and taken to the hospital, the truth didn't fully sink in. Arjun held her hand the entire time. The one time that Veera glanced at him, she saw that his eyes were clouded with grief. He was trying to be strong for her.

A strange hollowness had spread through her. She was aching to connect, to *process* what had happened, but her brain had shut down. All she could do was stare out the window without really seeing and think without really feeling.

Unconsciously, she started humming a song—an old *High School Musical* song—and just like that, the hurt punched her in the gut. So hard, she gasped out loud. It was one of Ananya's favourite songs and the thought that Ananya would never hear it again, that Veera would never hear it with Ananya again, ripped her heart into shreds. She dug her nails into Arjun's hand and squeezed her eyes shut, swallowing the tears that rose up in her throat.

The hospital loomed up in front of them, glaring-white and unwelcoming. As they entered the sterile building, Veera remembered how much Ananya hated hospitals.

'Why can't they be colourful and fun? Why do they have to be dull and claustrophobic?' Ananya used to argue.

Used to. Past tense.

'Veera,' Arjun was whispering urgently, his grip on her wrist vice-like. 'Maybe you shouldn't see her.'

She looked up. The bright fluorescent lights were blinding her. They were at the end of a long corridor. Her parents had gone ahead but Arjun was holding her back.

Fear clawed at her throat. He was right—she didn't want to see Ananya. Maybe if she didn't see her, then she could just go back home and pretend that none of this had happened. Her brain was still running on a lag.

Arjun's face softened, like he had guessed what was going on in her head. That look of pity, even from her own brother, was too much for Veera. In that moment, she hated everyone. She yanked her wrist out of his grip savagely and turned the corner.

Her stomach dropped as she took in the scene. She saw Ananya's mom, her pretty face marred by a cascade of tears. And then there was her dad, the picture of devastation. His hands were buried deep in his hair and he looked so broken. Veera's parents were sitting beside them, consoling them.

As if consoling them would ever bring their daughter back.

And in between all of them was a lump, hidden under layers of white blankets. Brown, wavy hair spilled from one end of the makeshift bed, but that was all the indication Veera needed.

Her breath caught. Before she knew it, she was kneeling beside the blanket-covered form, ripping the sheets off the lump.

And there she was—the one person she probably knew better than herself. Milky skin, full lips, wavy, brown hair, and eyes that would have been dark brown had they been open, framed by long, black lashes. Ananya lay still. Her chest neither rose nor fell.

She drew no breath.

Her heart didn't beat any more.

Reality slammed into Veera with the force of a truck. With a strangled cry, she scrambled for Ananya's hand. They were frozen but she held on to them for dear life.

'No . . .' The dam broke and the tears flowed down her face. Before she knew it, she was shaking Ananya, begging, pleading with her to get up. Feeling flooded back into her and the force of the pain made her see red. Fire coursed through her veins, her palm was burning against Ananya's cold, unmoving arm, her pulse thundered in her ear and everything around her exploded like a nuclear blast. Her best friend was lying lifeless in front of her.

She cried till she could cry no more, slumped on the cold hospital floor. When the tears ran out, she screamed till her throat was hoarse. Somewhere through the haze of pain, she was dimly aware of the word 'aneurysm' being tossed around by the people close to her. The word sounded alien to her ears—cold, metallic and completely unemotional. It sounded insensitive too, as if it hadn't just taken the life of someone who meant more than the world to her. But right then, it didn't matter. Nothing mattered.

After what seemed like years—when the spinning world around her had slowed to a methodical swaying and when she could lift her head without her brain feeling like it might explode—she groped in her bag for her phone.

Aneurysm.

She tasted the strange, metallic word as she typed it on Google search. Her eyes pricked, like more tears might flow, but none did. She was all maxed out.

Ananya was gone, and Veera was left learning the cause of her death on the Internet.

Kavya

Kavya sighed as she checked her reflection in the school bathroom. Although her uniform was impeccable as usual—skirt slightly shorter than necessary and hair done up in a high plait with a tiny pouf—she was worried about the bags under her eyes.

The result of crying her eyes out for the past two days.

Ananya. Oh my God, Ananya.

It had all happened so fast that Kavya barely had time to digest anything. Even when Aslesha had called her, bawling into the phone, it was the last thing Kavya had expected. She'd told her that Veera had been inconsolable and also completely unreachable. Aslesha had got the news from her parents.

She felt the familiar pricking behind her eyes that announced the arrival of tears. Ananya and Kavya hadn't exactly been the best of friends, but Ananya had always been there for her, no matter what. She couldn't say the same for herself, though.

With a groan, she passed her hand over her eyes to flick away a stray tear and walked out of the bathroom.

She entered XI C, her eyes scanning for Veera. It wasn't hard to spot her. She was sitting in their usual spot but was now surrounded by people—comforting her, offering their condolences and, most of all, wanting to know what had really happened. But Veera just sat there, oblivious to all those around her, with a vacant look in her eyes.

Aslesha was sitting next to her, doing all the explaining, and Siddharth sat next to her, clutching her hand.

Wait, what?

Why was Siddharth holding Veera's hand? Kavya stiffened. The nerve of that boy! First, he dumps her—Her! Who does that? Who in their right mind would dump Kavya Dhar?—and now he goes around gallivanting with other girls just to prove a point?

But this is Veera, a voice inside her head whispered. Kavya grimaced and made her way to the group.

'Yes, it's called an aneurysm. Virtually undetectable, and lethal if it bursts,' Aslesha was explaining, as Kavya took the seat beside her. 'Ananya had a brain aneurysm.'

'Guys!' a voice yelled. Kavya turned to see Shivani, one of her classmates. 'Oh my God, I can't believe it . . . I just heard about Ananya. I'm so sorry!' She raced towards them, her arms open wide for a hug.

Kavya got up to receive the hug but Shivani raced right past her and hugged Veera, who barely responded. Kavya grimaced.

This happened *all the time*. All everyone wanted to know was how Veera was doing and if she was fine. They wanted to hear about what had happened to Ananya only from Veera; they sympathized with Veera alone. All anyone ever spoke about was the pain Veera was suffering.

Kavya was Ananya's friend too, for God's sake! Nobody wanted to know how she was feeling. Nobody was paying her any attention. It was always about Veera! Even when she was crying herself hoarse over the past two days, nobody had been there for her.

When Kavya had confronted Aslesha about this, things hadn't really gone as smoothly as she had hoped they would.

'Don't be such a kid, Kavya, it isn't always about you,' Aslesha had said coldly. Kavya bit her lip in anger. Trust Aslesha to always hurt you with the truth.

'But you weren't there for me! You were with Veera!' Kavya had whined.

'You should've been with her too. But you wanted to grieve alone, so we let you.' There was a weary look in Aslesha's eyes. 'I'm begging you, Kavya, just for a few days, try not to create a scene just because others are getting a little more attention than you are.'

Whatever.

Now Kavya looked around at the lunchtime scene in XI C and felt suffocated. Her eyes flickered to Siddharth momentarily. He hadn't even acknowledged her presence.

'I'll be back,' she said, but hardly anyone heard.

She turned on her heel and walked out of the class. She'd let the others handle the drama.

Her thoughts wandered as she walked aimlessly down the school hallway. In the past few days, she had neither eaten nor gone out. She'd stayed shut in her room, bundled up inside her blanket, and cried her heart out. Kavya was a cry-er . . . she cried for the smallest things.

Ananya was the constant in their group. The rock, the person who was always there for everyone. Regardless of what fight you were in, if you needed her, she would be there. But if you crossed her, she wouldn't forget for a long time. Ananya was far from being a saint. In fact, she could be vicious, but that didn't take away from the fact that she was an amazing friend. She took friendships so damn seriously . . . it was always all or nothing with her. How in the world could she possibly be gone?

Kavya rounded the corner and her eyes widened at what she saw.

A boy was standing on top of the parapet that surrounded the corridors and looking down at the courtyard. There was no railing, nor was there any other means of support—he was about one strong gust of wind away from tumbling to his death.

Kavya yelped in surprise, her hands going to her heart. She glanced around quickly to make sure no one was around.

'Nikhil?' she stage-whispered, her heart hammering. 'What are you doing up there?'

Nikhil turned around slowly and Kavya held back a frown. He looked dreadful, like he hadn't slept for days. There were bags under his eyes and the knuckles on his right hand looked bruised.

'Just thinking,' he deadpanned.

'Can't you think from down here?' Kavya said urgently. 'Some teacher will see you! Or worse, you could fall down, you idiot!'

'It would be nice to.' Nikhil regarded her coolly. 'Fall down, I mean.'

27

Kavya rolled her eyes. Even though they were in the same group, Nikhil and Kavya were hardly close. They were friends who had fun together, not friends who had deep conversations and knew each other's issues. She remembered Ananya mentioning how gloomy and dark Nikhil could get, but she was in no mood to deal with other people's problems right now.

Ironic, since you want others to deal with your drama all the time, the little voice in her head whispered. Kavya sighed, exasperated. She wished she could turn off her mind sometimes. That voice inside her was becoming progressively more annoying.

'Can you at least sit down? You're making me nervous,' Kavya said. Realizing that she had nothing better to do right then, she hauled herself up on to the parapet and patted the spot next to her, looking up at Nikhil.

'What, no rapping today?' she asked dryly. Nikhil didn't even crack a smile. 'I'm guessing you heard about . . .'

Nikhil didn't respond. He just sat down and looked away. After a long silence, Kavya couldn't handle it any more and prepared to walk away. Just as she was about to jump off, Nikhil spoke.

'She mattered more to me than any of you'll know.'

Kavya stopped, curious. Nikhil and Ananya had always been close. But no one had ever known how and why.

'Did you . . . um . . . like her or something?' Kavya asked, cocking an eyebrow.

Nikhil gave her his you've-got-to-be-kidding-me look.

Kavya shrugged. 'Fine, fine, it was just a question, geez!'

'She actually understood me. No, not in that girly, cliché sort of way. She saw *me*, the real me.' He pointed to his heart.

'And she didn't leave. She knew what a pain in the ass I could be and she tried to make things better . . . while the rest of you barely tolerated me.'

He held up a hand when Kavya opened her mouth to protest. 'Don't even deny it.' So Kavya didn't deny it.

After a bit of silence, Kavya snorted. 'You know, it's funny how everyone makes Ananya out to be such a saint after she's . . . you know . . .'

'It's obligatory,' Nikhil replied, not at all affected by Kavya's perspective. 'Be a bitch to her when she's alive and now that she's not there, let's all say nice things about her. People are always like that . . . That's why I avoid people. She was a strong person and sometimes the only way to be strong is to act like you don't care about anything . . . or anyone.'

Kavya looked at Nikhil. Part of her scoffed at all the pretentious rubbish he was spouting. But a tiny part of her couldn't help wondering if he was talking about Ananya or himself.

'I'm her best friend too—' Kavya started.

'Were. You *were* her friend.' Nikhil winced.

For a minute the sadness struck her with renewed vigour. It was so easy to forget that there was no Ananya any more. As tears threatened to overwhelm her, she swallowed forcefully and continued.

'I was her best friend too, and no one asked me how I'm doing. It's all Veera-this and Veera-that.' The moment she said the words, she wanted to take them back. She realized how childish and insensitive they sounded. She bit her lips and waited for the lecture that she was about to get.

It never came.

'God, you really *are* horrible,' Nikhil chuckled softly. There was no venom in his voice.

Kavya's eyes narrowed. 'And that doesn't bother you because . . .?'

Nikhil raised an eyebrow. 'I'm hardly one to judge. What goes on here,' he said, tapping his temple, 'is worse than what goes on there.' He tapped the side of her head.

Wow. Normally, anyone who dared to call her horrible would immediately have been struck off her friends list and a vicious round of back-biting would have followed. But funnily enough, she wasn't offended when Nikhil said it. He'd just said it in a matter-of-fact way, simple and non-judgemental.

'Oh, come on, your thoughts can't really be *that* dark,' Kavya muttered. 'All that brooding, gloomy vibe is cool and all, but seriously, it's getting old.'

'I'm messed up in so many ways . . . and Ananya understood,' Nikhil almost whispered. 'But she's gone and there is no one who understands me any more.'

Kavya resisted the urge to roll her eyes. *So says every teenager on this planet—I can't be fixed*, she thought to herself.

'How do you mean, messed up?' she asked out loud, just as the bell trilled to announce the end of lunch break.

Nikhil looked around, then jumped off the parapet and dusted his pants.

'That's a story for another time, I've to get to class.' He turned to walk away, leaving Kavya, still sitting on the parapet.

'Aren't you even going to offer to help me down?' Kavya asked, almost offended.

'No!' Nikhil looked surprised, like it never even occurred to him. Kavya made a face and jumped down.

'Wait!' she shouted as Nikhil turned. 'We're in the same class! I'll come with you, tell me on the way.'

Nikhil let out a short but genuine laugh. 'Did you consider that maybe I don't want to tell you?'

An amused smile tugged at his lips as he turned and walked away, leaving a very confused and embarrassed Kavya still rooted to the same spot.

Siddharth

Siddharth had met Ananya in kindergarten, a time when it was acceptable for boys and girls to be just friends. She had been the new kid then, and the students in their class had readily accepted her as one of their own.

Being the gentleman that he was, he had invited her to sit next to him and join his small group. Within the next hour, all introductions had been made and Siddharth had finished pointing out whom Ananya should talk to and whom she should avoid—because they 'never share their crayons'. Ananya had nodded vigorously at this, since even she knew that not sharing crayons was cruelty of the worst kind.

Ananya soon found herself in the middle of an animated conversation about Power Rangers, Pokemons and Beyblades, which had been all the rage at the time. Siddharth had been mighty impressed when, instead of grimacing like all the other girls and walking away, she had whole-heartedly joined the discussion. It was soon evident that Ananya's knowledge in these matters far exceeded half the boys' in her class.

From that day on, Ananya and Siddharth became Power Ranger best friends. They were inseparable. All their breaks would be spent re-enacting scenes from the series (where

Ananya would always be Pink Ranger and Siddharth, Red Ranger) or trading precious Pokemon cards in the shadowy corners of the corridors with the stealth and efficiency of the CIA.

Sometimes the best friendships are built on the simplest foundations and maybe that's why their friendship stood the test of time, although it wasn't always easy.

After kindergarten came primary and then middle school, where it gradually became uncool for boys to hang out with girls. Siddharth remembered those years, when the conversations he had with Ananya were brief and pointless and pretty much just a formality. He made friends with more boys his age and started playing football. In the meantime, Ananya found herself mixing with the popular-girl crowd, the kind that dressed like they were eighteen but had the mental age of three.

If things had gone on the same way, it would have been very hard for Siddharth and Ananya to reconnect. When they hit their tweens, guy-girl friendships were back in vogue, but it was hardly the same. If a boy and girl were friends, people were always looking for it to evolve into something more. Rumours ran riot and gossip spread like wildfire. Siddharth rolled his eyes at how juvenile all of it was.

'Whom do you like?'

Four short words that summarized the game of Truth or Dare perfectly. Siddharth remembered this one game of T or D particularly well. It was a game that he himself hadn't taken part in, but it had nevertheless made him laugh. When Ananya had been pressured by her gang of girls to answer this question, she had quickly blurted out his name to shut everyone up. She was embarrassed beyond measure, especially since she and Siddharth had barely spoken in the past few years. But when she'd told him about it, Siddharth had just been extremely amused.

'Why would you say that?' he had laughed, looking at the red-faced Ananya.

'God, I felt so put on the spot, I had to tell them *something*! Otherwise they would have never stopped hounding me,' she had replied, cringing.

The idea of liking Ananya as anything more than a friend was preposterous and he knew that she felt the same way. Of course, she was way more than a friend in many ways, but never in *that* way. She was his best adviser, his sister, and even though she was older than him by a few months, he felt protective of her in some ways—like she was his ward. In his mind, there was only a thin, almost indistinguishable, line separating her from being family.

Then, in secondary school, Ananya and Siddharth were in the same class once more and had an opportunity to become as close as they used to be. He had sighed with relief as he watched Ananya step out from the shadow of the 'popular' clique and carve a name for herself as an intelligent and effective writer.

It was around the same time that Siddharth developed a huge crush on Kavya and approached Ananya and Veera, Kavya's best friends then, to help him out.

It was always a little glamorous to play matchmaker—it made you feel wanted, brought drama into the life of everyone concerned and became a precious school memory. And so Veera and Ananya had agreed. It was a win-win situation for all—Siddharth got Kavya and also had Ananya back in his life.

But now, just like that, Ananya was not in his life any more. And nothing he did would ever bring her back.

'Siddharth!'

The water in his glass sloshed around a little as he turned.

Ananya's house displayed a riot of colours and smells, all mixed together with a chorus of a dozen people talking. In the middle, a *havankund* had been erected around which priests sat, performing the thirteenth-day rites.

It had already been thirteen days, thirteen unbearable days, since Ananya had been gone. Muffled laughter echoed through the house. It was by no means a solemn occasion, since the thirteenth day was supposed to be a day of joy, to pray for the journey of the soul to the other side. It was now appropriate for far-off relatives and not-so-close friends to come out of formal mourning. But today was just a meaningless ritual for all those who felt true grief.

'Mahir.' Siddharth would have been happy to see one of his best friends had it been under different circumstances. He grimaced inwardly. Mahir had just returned from a fortnight-long football camp that started the day Ananya had died.

Without any pretence, Mahir grabbed Siddharth's shoulder. 'Please,' he almost whispered. 'Tell me it's not true.' The dull-gold sherwani he wore was crumpled, like he had put it on in a hurry, and his forehead was creased with worry.

'I wish I could,' Siddharth said, steeling himself. 'It's the thirteenth day today, how did you know you needed to come here?' He pointed around at the surroundings.

Mahir swore loudly, his voice cracking, and sat down on the floor with his head in his hands. 'Mom . . . but I was hoping it was some sick joke . . . or . . . or . . . *anything*—except this!'

Siddharth sighed. He was dealing with the loss so far, mainly because he had put off handling his pain. His mom had told him that he was in denial. Honestly, he couldn't have cared less. Helping other people cope with their grief made it easier for him to delay the pain he would undoubtedly feel, left to himself.

'Get up, man.' Siddharth offered his hand and Mahir got up.

'How . . . She was fine the day I saw her,' Mahir spluttered. 'She . . . I wanted . . . urgh! I don't know how to explain what I'm feeling.'

Without meaning to, Siddharth snorted. Mahir's head shot up. 'What?'

'No offence, but it didn't look like she mattered much to you. It doesn't feel like anything matters much to you these days—except those clingy girls that you so obviously keep leading on! Ananya was never part of your life, man . . . She tried to keep the friendship alive, but you were too busy keeping your popularity alive,' Siddharth lashed out.

Mahir took a step back, as though slapped. 'Where is this coming from?' he asked incredulously. 'You don't believe that I cared for Ananya?'

'Forgive me if I don't,' Siddharth replied coldly. He knew he was being difficult, not to mention completely ridiculous, but he didn't care. It was hard to sympathize with Mahir when it was so obvious that he hadn't given two hoots about Ananya when she was alive, and now that she was no longer there, here he was, pretending to know her *so* well. 'I know you, Mahir.'

'See, that's the thing.' Mahir stepped closer. 'Nobody knows about me and Ananya. *Nobody.*' And with that, he turned and stalked off.

Siddharth felt guilty, but also instantly defensive. If nobody knew about him and Ananya, then was their friendship real at all? Her *real* friends were Veera, Aslesha, Kavya, Nikhil, him, Aakash—*oh my God, Aakash!*

If anybody was in worse shape than Veera, it was Aakash. That dude was a broken man. For the past thirteen days he had avoided everybody. He hadn't eaten, looked like he hadn't slept and barely spoke a word. He had shut himself off so completely, even Siddharth was having trouble reaching out to him.

Feeling a hand on his shoulder, he turned.

'Oh, hi Uncle.' Siddharth looked into the tired face of Ananya's father. He wondered how sick it was that this guy had to attend his own daughter's funeral.

Ananya's father gave him a watery smile. 'Listen, Siddharth, have you seen Veera by any chance?' When Siddharth shook his head, he continued. 'Do me a favour and go look for her, will you? It's not good for her to be alone . . . in the state she's in.'

Siddharth understood. But he also knew that Veera wouldn't do anything stupid. She absolutely *detested* self-harm. But he nodded enthusiastically at Uncle. He was glad that he had something to do.

He quickly waved to Ananya's dad and turned. The house wasn't huge but it wasn't small either. Good thing he already had an idea where Veera might be.

As he made his way around the house, he found himself thinking about Ananya's father. Ananya always said that he and Siddharth were so alike. Maybe that's why she knew exactly how to handle Siddharth at his worst. Maybe that's also why Ananya could anger Siddharth quicker than anybody else.

Most of their fights had been about one thing—Siddharth's constant mingling.

He sighed, running a hand through his hair, as he remembered one argument that had irked him in particular.

'Why do you have to go with them?' Ananya questioned Siddharth one day when they were hanging out at her house.

'We've been over this, Ananya!' Siddharth huffed. He sat down on the sofa and looked at her, exasperated. 'They are my friends too! Why can't I hang out with them?'

'But you're in OUR group!' Ananya shot back.

'I'm in THEIR group TOO!' Siddharth yelled. 'Can you stop doing this every time? I hate feeling so . . . restrained!'

'Restrained,' Ananya echoed his last word. Then she bit her lip and looked away.

Siddharth sighed. Great, now Ananya was upset.

He hated these arguments.

But it was true. Okay, maybe 'restrained' was too strong a word, but he knew that Ananya and the others were definitely unhappy with the fact that he hung out with other people. And Siddharth hated this 'clique' business. He liked talking to all sorts of people.

'Ananya.' He tugged at her hand. She didn't turn. After a few more tugs, she finally looked at him. 'Come on, you know I didn't mean that . . . I didn't mean it like that, at least.'

He expected more accusations, more sarcasm, more anger. But Ananya just collapsed beside him on the sofa, her anger crumbling.

'I know,' she sighed, scraping her hair back into a neat ponytail. That was her tell, a nervous tic. She played with her hair every time she was under stress. 'It's just . . .'

'Just what?' Siddharth looked at her with amusement. For a person who was so good with words, Ananya sure had trouble expressing her feelings out loud.

'Nothing, forget it. It makes me look clingy,' she huffed, combing her ponytail with her fingers.

Siddharth sighed mockingly. 'Ananya, I don't think it's humanly possible for someone to be clingier than you—OW!' He winced as Ananya smacked him. 'Just spit it out.'

'Fine,' Ananya exhaled dramatically. 'I don't like to think that you have more fun with other people.'

Siddharth raised an eyebrow . . . and burst out laughing. 'What are you, my girlfriend?'

Ananya didn't bat an eyelid. 'You wish.'

'You're right, that was SO clingy.'

'Siddharth Ahuja, this is the last freaking time I'm telling you any of my true feelings!' Then she got up and started to stomp off.

He was up in a jiffy and had both her arms locked behind her back. As she squirmed under his hold, she screamed, 'Let me go, you idiot!'

Siddharth loosened his grip and Ananya kicked him in the shin. As he collapsed on to the carpet, he dragged her down, and soon they both were lying on the floor, laughing.

After catching his breath, Siddharth managed to wheeze out, 'No, but really, you wouldn't have said those words even in your dreams. You might've felt them, thought them, but you would never utter those words! Seriously?'

'Okay, those weren't my words exactly,' Ananya said sheepishly, and after Siddharth shot her an I-have-zero-patience-right-now look, she rolled her eyes and said, 'Fine—Veera might've mentioned it. But that's not the point.'

It made perfect sense. He knew Veera thought that, but why did it still sting so much? He didn't know how to make these girls understand that he had two types of friends in his life—friends and I-would-do-anything-for-them friends. Yeah, well, he could be extreme. Either you were significant in Siddharth's life, or you weren't. Simple. Ananya and Veera fell in the second category, but he didn't know how to make them realize this and that irritated him.

'The others—my football friends, the people from the various school clubs—that I hang out with,' he started slowly, 'are not competition.' He looked straight at Ananya till she nodded. Both of them were aware that he was actually answering Veera.

'No one—and I'm dead serious when I say NO ONE—is going to, or will ever, replace you guys, okay?' And Siddharth knew, even as he said it, that he truly meant it.

'I'm with you guys because I like it, because y'all are like my weird, annoying family. And the best part about family is that we don't have to spend every second of every day together to make sure that we stay close, right? Now this conversation is getting too mushy for my liking, so can we please go have ice cream so that I can feel tough and manly again?'

'How is ice cream going to make you feel manly?' Ananya laughed.

'Excuse me, ice cream is like the manliest food ever! Now are you coming or not?'

A sharp knock pulled him back to the present. It was a few moments before he registered that he was standing in front of Ananya's closed room and it was his knuckles rapping on the door.

The door was flung open and Siddharth almost stumbled back in shock. 'Woah!'

'Really? I look that bad?' Veera's face was blank, like her face had forgotten how to produce different expressions. Only a light, teasing note in her voice showed a faint trace of the old Veera.

'NO!' Siddharth said, then grimaced at his enthusiasm. 'I mean, no . . . it's not . . . wow, it's the opposite, actually.'

Veera's eyebrow rose a fraction of an inch—she didn't believe Siddharth in the least. 'It's okay, you can say I look like crap, you know.'

Siddharth shook his head vigorously, smoothing his sherwani. She looked anything but bad. Of course, he had seen Veera dressed-up, but he had never seen her in traditional Indian clothes before.

He couldn't stop himself giving her a once-over. She had a spectacular figure because of her Bharatanatyam classes. She was wearing a peacock-blue south Indian half-sari with a gold border. Her neck was bare, with just her collarbone arching like a bow, and she wore blue rings in her ears. Her large eyes were thickly lined with kajal and there was the slightest tinge of pink on her lips.

She looked so simple but so . . . breathtaking.

Right then, Veera cleared her throat and the spell broke. Shit! He realized with a start that he had been staring. He turned away quickly, his face hot.

Wait, what?

Did he just *blush?*

'So . . .' Veera continued to look at him and he realized that he hadn't responded to her previous statement.

'You look beautiful,' he said without thinking.

If Siddharth could have killed himself right then, he would have. And in the most painful way. Beautiful? *Beautiful?* WHAT WAS HE THINKING! There were a hundred other adjectives that he could've used—pretty, hot . . . hell, even 'nice' would've been all right. But *nooooooo!*

'Beautiful' was a pretty big word.

What's the big deal? Siddharth thought. *It's not like you meant anything by it.*

You so totally did! Another voice inside his head laughed.

Shut up, he grumbled inwardly.

'Um . . . thanks?' Veera replied, slightly flustered. That was not what she'd expected.

'So . . . they were, umm, looking for you outside,' Siddharth stammered. *Total lie.*

'Oh.' Veera walked into the room, beckoning Siddharth to come in and shut the door. 'Does it make me incredibly selfish when I say that I don't want to go out?'

'No, not really,' Siddharth said, shutting the door behind him. 'It's kind of depressing out there. Especially when people actually expect you to make small talk.'

Ananya's room was completely pink and white, but it somehow managed to look sophisticated, and not like it belonged to some hyperactive five-year-old. Even after thirteen days, the room looked completely lived in, like Ananya would just stroll in any time. Her bed was creased, her pillows slightly askew. Her laptop lay on her desk, papers with half-finished writing were spread out on her bay window and a few clothes lay on the floor beneath her mirror. Ananya had probably left them there after trying them on.

'I can't talk about it,' Veera said. 'I can't even accept it. Every part of my body is *screaming* that there must be some way to bring her back, but my stupid, *stupid* brain knows it's not possible.'

Siddharth didn't know what to say, so he sat beside her on Ananya's bed.

'I saw it. I *saw* my best friend dead in front of me.' Veera's voice trembled. 'And it was like, in that moment, my entire world just crashed. How am I supposed to live through that?'

Siddharth was quiet. Probably thinking his silence was out of awkwardness, Veera backtracked hurriedly.

'I'm sorry. I shouldn't be unloading all of this on you . . . Seriously, this is not your issue—'

'Because you're Veera.' Siddharth looked at her finally. 'You asked me how you're supposed to live through this. You'll survive it because you are Veera. You're the strongest girl I know. I suck at this whole consoling thing—but I know that you'll get through this. And I'll be here the whole time.'

'Why?' Her voice was almost a whisper.

Siddharth shrugged. 'Because I'm your "second best friend",' he said, referring to the childish phrase.

'Thanks.' A ghost of a smile flickered on her face. And as suddenly as it had appeared, it vanished. 'What's that?' she asked, pointing.

Siddharth's eyes followed her finger. Veera was pointing to a spot above a cabinet on the wall. On top of the cabinet, nearly hidden from view, was a tiny blue shoebox.

Intrigued, Siddharth dragged the chair from her study table and retrieved it carefully, handing it over to Veera. Her hands shook as she took it from him. The box was surprisingly light.

'Open it.' Siddharth nudged Veera.

Hesitating for only a moment, Veera whipped the lid off, exposing its contents.

Inside, in neat piles, were seven creamy envelopes. Siddharth was itching to open them but he waited while Veera examined them first. She picked up the topmost one and turned it over. Her forehead creased with confusion as she saw what was written.

On the back of the envelope, was Veera's name, written in blood-red ink, followed by a date.

'Is there one addressed to me?' Siddharth asked. He was dying of curiosity. Together they removed the letters from the box and spread them out on the wooden floor.

'There's one for each of us . . . you, me, Kavya, Aslesha, Nikhil, Aakash . . . and Mahir. Our names followed by a date. And as far as I can make out, the dates are random,' Siddharth said, frowning. 'What *are* these?' He was completely nonplussed.

'Letters,' Veera breathed. Her fingers traced the writing on each envelope fondly. They were written by Ananya, whose handwriting was probably as familiar to her as her own, Siddharth figured. The looping of the 'l's, the tiny dotted 'i's and the hurriedly crossed 't's. Veera looked up at Siddharth, her eyes shining.

'But . . .' Siddharth was more cautious. 'She couldn't possibly have known about the aneurysm.'

'Who said these were death letters? They could just be stuff she wrote. Look.' Veera held up the lid of the shoebox. On the underside of the lid was a large neon-yellow Post-it with Ananya's familiar scrawl.

This note is for me since the contents of these letters are never going to be read by anyone else. In the unlikely event that I should ever lose my memory or some rubbish like that, this note will serve as a reminder. Hahahaha! I'm hilarious. Kidding, kidding. It's just more glamorous that way.

These letters are my outlet to vent and rant. Maybe I can't say these things to you guys, maybe I'm dying to tell you these things but haven't found the right time . . . maybe one day I'll even give y'all these (not happening). But until then, hopefully, they'll remain undiscovered . . . I hide them in plain sight because I saw that trick in a movie once. Apparently they won't be discovered that way.

Mom, if you're reading this, please don't read the letters. In all of them I have spoken the ABSOLUTE truth, since I wrote them thinking they won't be read. But I'm not naive enough to believe that they will never be discovered. All I hope is that it's later rather than sooner. Urgh! It would be so embarrassing if you saw this . . . I'm so damn emotional in them.

Any other nosy person:
1. Keep the box back calmly and no one gets hurt.
2. Get the hell out of my room!

Ananya Krishnan (peace!)

Siddharth whistled softly. 'You've got to be kidding me. She's crazy! Who the hell writes letters that they don't plan to send? That's so *The Notebook*!'

'If I remember correctly, the guy actually *did* send the letters, she just didn't get them.' Veera's eyes hadn't lost their recent sparkle. 'Let's call the rest of the group. We have to give them these letters.'

Siddharth stared at her incredulously. 'Are you sure that's a good idea?' The truth was that he didn't want to be in the same room as Kavya.

'Can you just be a man and deal with your break-up already?' Veera rolled her eyes, startling Siddharth. He looked at her and smiled. The edge in her voice made him happy. To hell with the consequences—the letters had given Veera a distraction, a temporary purpose, and who was he to deny her that?

'I'll call the rest.'

He didn't know what the plan was, but he trusted Veera enough to let her do what she wanted.

Veera

The tension in the room was making it hard to breathe. Veera fidgeted continuously with the hem of her pallu. Siddharth stood at her side, in front of his friends, staring stonily at the wall ahead, avoiding their eyes.

Veera felt a surge of anger at the unease in the room. All of them were like family; they had known each other for years and now, just because they had barely interacted with each other over the past two weeks, there was suddenly so much awkwardness in the air. It was almost as if Ananya's death had fractured the group.

'Awkward silence,' Kavya said in her sing-song voice, and a couple of people in the room rolled their eyes.

Veera looked at everyone. Kavya wore a carefully crafted mask of boredom but Veera knew that behind that mask she was hurting. Just like the rest of them. Aslesha looked restless and wouldn't look anyone in the eye, like she had to constantly do something to keep her mind off Ananya. Nikhil's mood was dark, as usual, and Aakash looked distraught. He hadn't raised his head even once.

As Veera's eyes skimmed over everyone's faces, they came to rest on Mahir's. His clothes were crumpled and his hair was standing up in all directions. He lifted his head to meet her gaze. Veera quickly looked away, her heart thudding.

Mahir was her ex. Before he had become the popular asshole he was now, he had been friends with Veera and Ananya. Veera and Mahir had lasted a whole year. But that's all. After that they had gradually started growing apart, until they finally decided to end it. As they started hanging out with different groups, they barely even knew what the other was up to. It was only because Siddharth was friends with Mahir and because of Ananya's weird involvement with him that she knew the bare minimum about his life. Veera knew that she was over him, but they never did manage to become friends after breaking up. And that made this entire situation weirder still.

'What's the matter? Why am I here?' Mahir finally asked what everyone was probably wondering.

Veera tensed. How was she supposed to explain this? Till now, she hadn't been able to talk about Ananya. Not to her parents, not to her friends, not to anyone.

'I can't do this,' she whispered to herself, but Siddharth heard her. Silently he slipped his hand into hers and gave it a reassuring squeeze. He didn't look at her but she saw the encouraging smile on his face.

Veera almost jumped at the sudden contact. For some reason, the warm pressure of his hand put her on edge. Shaking her head, she gripped his hand like it was her only connection to the world and plunged into the inevitable explanation.

As she spoke, the eyebrows in the room rose higher and higher. But no one doubted Veera for a second. Yes, this was dramatic, but also exactly like something Ananya would do.

'They were all written on random dates. I don't know their content. But they're addressed to each of us. It's—' Her voice broke as she distributed the letters. 'It's all we have left of her.'

'These are all dated almost a year back,' Aslesha observed, studying the letter gravely.

'Yup,' Veera nodded. 'What I was thinking is that maybe we could open it on the same dates that these were written on in the coming year. It seems fitting somehow—unless, of course, you guys want to do something different?'

No one objected to her idea so Veera took that as a yes.

'Yup,' Siddharth spoke for the first time. 'Let's not break this pact. We do not need to reveal the contents to anyone. If you don't want to open it, then don't . . . it's up to you.'

'Okay . . . if that is all, then I'm leaving. I only came here for Ananya, otherwise I don't give a damn about these religious customs,' Nikhil said, getting up.

All of them smiled at this and exchanged glances. And just like that, the tension was diffused. No explanations were made, no condolences offered, no hugs, nothing. But Veera knew that they would be there for each other through this horribly difficult time.

'We know all about your atheism, thank you very much,' Siddharth grinned, as everyone filed out of the room.

'It is what it is.' Nikhil gave a glum smile before leaving. Veera waited patiently till everyone had exited.

After the door shut behind Aakash, Veera looked at the letter in her hand. It suddenly seemed way too heavy for a simple piece of paper. She traced her thumb over her name, calligraphed on the envelope. Even Ananya's handwriting brought back memories. She felt the familiar burning in the back of her throat that announced the arrival of tears and clenched her fists.

She. Would. Not. Cry.

Most definitely not in front of Siddharth.

Before she could turn and walk out of the room to find a quiet corner in the house, Siddharth spoke.

'Veera! Hey, are you okay?'

No. 'Yeah, I'm fine.'

'Let's try that again, and let's try not to lie this time, shall we? Are you okay?'

Veera raised her eyes to meet his. 'Yes, I'm fine. Now please stop asking me that.'

The unnecessary venom in her voice made her wince. But if Siddharth kept this up, she knew she would cave. And once the tears started, God only knew when they would stop.

'Tell me what's wrong.'

'Nothing! Nothing is wrong! I'm going to go outside and try and help out.'

She whirled around and started walking to the door. But she had barely taken two steps, when Siddharth caught her wrist and pulled her back.

'Come here.' He pulled her closer with an exasperated sigh.

In a second, his arms were around her, protective, comforting. She was crushed against him in a warm hug and suddenly, all the walls that she'd built around herself in the past two weeks came crashing down. Pain squeezed her insides so hard that she instinctively clutched his sherwani. His hands tightened around her. She buried her head in the crook of his neck and tried to disappear in his embrace.

As she breathed in his fresh, lemony smell, she was suddenly *very* aware of his arms around her. The pressure of his hands on the small of her back, her out-of-control heartbeat, the rise and fall of his chest . . . but what startled her most was the realization that for the first time since Ananya's death, she felt safe. Her mind was grounded, anchored to the present.

'It's okay to cry once in a while, you know,' Siddharth whispered.

Veera shook her head, not meeting his eyes. 'Your sherwani will get wet.'

Siddharth's chest vibrated against her as he laughed quietly. 'Seriously? You're worried about my sherwani? Just cry, it's okay.'

And so Veera did. She didn't bawl, but she cried quietly, completely. And the entire time, he held her, uncomplainingly. As her sobs receded to hiccups, she felt his fingers in her hair, stroking it softly.

'You seem to be handling this unbelievably well; most people don't know how to deal with bawling girls,' Veera sniffed, attempting a smile. 'How many people have you ambushed like this?' she asked, referring to the hug.

'Not many,' Siddharth said, resting his chin on her head and swaying gently. 'None actually . . . you are the first.'

Veera's eyebrows shot up and she twisted in an attempt to look at him, upsetting his chin in the process. 'Kavya?'

Siddharth made an exasperated noise. 'Can you not? My chin needs something to rest on, please don't move—thank you—and Kavya . . . she never even let me come close enough to hold her hand, let alone comfort her.'

Veera chuckled. She could get used to this. It wasn't the least bit awkward; they were behaving like they did this all the time. That startled Veera more than anything else. But for the moment she let it slide. She was content to just stay like that for some more time. And since Siddharth wasn't showing any indication of pulling away, she laid her head on his chest again.

'I told you not to move—' Siddharth started, just as the door opened with a bang.

'I had just—oh.'

'Kavya!' Veera said, wrenching herself away from Siddharth even as he let her go suddenly. She was desperately hoping that Kavya hadn't seen them together.

All such illusions were dispelled the moment Kavya spoke.

'I'm sorry. I had forgotten my bag here . . . but clearly I interrupted something . . . important.' Her tone was icy. She walked stiffly to where her golden clutch—a sparkly little thing—lay and, after securing its strap around her wrist, stomped out.

Veera shot Siddharth a helpless look.

'Kavya, wait!' Veera shouted.

Kavya stopped at the door. 'Don't bother,' she growled. And she slammed the door shut.

'You don't have to justify yourself. You did nothing wrong!' Siddharth said, sensing Veera's thoughts.

Veera rubbed her forehead, still staring after Kavya. 'N-no. I'm supposed to be one of her best friends and you're her . . . ex. This goes against every friend code that ever existed.'

'Why, there's nothing going on between us. Nothing happened.'

To her surprise, she felt her heart sink. Why was she disappointed? He was right—nothing really had happened . . . And here she was, her heart thudding like the fool it was.

Convincing herself that it was her nerves and the mixed emotions of the day that were making her feel this way, she turned to face him.

'I have to go, she'll be fuming now.'

Siddharth nodded as Veera walked to the door. 'But thanks,' she said, looking back at him. 'I really needed that.'

She turned the handle, and just before she shut the door behind her, Siddharth called out, 'Just so you know, I don't regret it.'

Her lips twitched upward in a faint half-smile.

'Me neither.'

'Will you listen to me!' Veera yanked at Kavya's elbow, preventing her from walking away. 'There is nothing, nothing going on between me and Siddharth. He's just a friend.'

'Do your guy friends normally comfort you that way?' Kavya demanded.

Veera sighed exasperatedly. 'Look past yourself for once, will you? I am attending my best friend's thirteenth-day ceremony. He was just comforting me, nothing else!'

'Wow, that's cool! Playing the my-best-friend-just-died-please-give-me-attention card! Poor little Veera. Always such a saint. SHE WAS MY BEST FRIEND TOO!' Kavya yelled.

Veera staggered back, stung. 'What? Where is this coming from?'

'Don't deny it. You *love* the attention,' Kavya spat.

Anger flared up inside Veera. She was defending herself in front of Kavya for something that she had no need to explain. Was it even possible for someone to be that incredibly, *stupidly* thick and insensitive? And now . . . how dare she say that Veera was enjoying the attention she got because of Ananya's death.

'If you stepped out of your own little world for two seconds, Kavya, you would probably be less of an absolute bitch. Loving the attention is *your* thing. I came to apologize even though I've done nothing wrong, but clearly you have more problems with me than just Siddharth. And I don't have time for this right now,' Veera said calmly.

Kavya rolled her eyes but froze as Veera stepped closer.

'But I'll tell you this—don't you dare turn Ananya's death into a shallow competition for attention.' And with that she turned and stalked away, anger coursing through her every vein.

Mahir

The blast from the AC hit him in the face as soon as Mahir stepped into the school hall. Students sat on the red plastic chairs laid out in neat rows, and the place buzzed with excited voices.

An assembly had been called, which in itself wasn't so uncommon. But then he'd heard the whispered conversations of the teachers and the prefect body as they rushed around trying to get things done. Something important—but last-minute—was scheduled for today.

He quickly spotted Siddharth in the sea of white and blue and slipped into the vacant seat next to him.

'What's going on?' he asked. Siddharth shrugged his shoulders in confusion.

A sudden hush spread through the hall. Mahir turned around and spotted their principal walking down the aisle towards the front of the hall. Mrs Vritika Deshmukh was a tall, stately lady, dressed in an elegant suit. Her hair was scraped back in a tight bun. She was a known perfectionist and was ultra-strict. Mahir rolled his eyes at the absolute silence that always followed in her wake. He wasn't exactly her most favourite student. Considering how many times he'd been reprimanded by her for his 'unruly conduct', he was quite sure he knew the inside of her office better than she did.

The tapping of a microphone pulled his attention to the front of the hall. A nervous teacher (must be someone from the primary section, for Mahir was unable to identify her) stood holding the mic, her eyes trained on the principal and the fakest of smiles stretched across her face.

'Children! Today our dear principal would like to address you all. Let's give her a round of applause.'

Next to him, Siddharth sat up straighter. 'I wonder what's up?'

The students clapped mechanically as she took the microphone from the teacher with a smile of acknowledgement. She then turned to face the students and held up one hand. The applause died down almost immediately. Her eyes swept over the entire hall, resting on each student for a millisecond, before she cleared her throat.

'Namaste, students.' She paused, waiting for them to respond in kind. Once they did, she resumed, 'I'm sure you're all wondering why I've called this assembly. In fact, I'm told that we had one just yesterday, right after your vacation.'

Mahir snorted. By 'vacation' she meant a three-day weekend.

'It is a very sad time for Agastya International,' VD continued. 'As you are all aware, one of our brilliant students—Ananya Krishnan—passed away on 15 November 2015. Following tradition, we observed a moment of silence and prayed for her soul in our classes, but now that we're all here, let us honour her memory together.'

Mahir sat bolt upright in his seat and could sense Siddharth tense up as well. *You've got to be kidding me.* Mahir and Siddharth exchanged a glance, their fists clenched, as they realized what was to follow.

An unnatural hush swept through the hall. The junior classes stood up to look at Ananya's friends, who averted their eyes angrily. All of the eleventh sighed in unison. *Couldn't the school just leave it alone?*

Taking the sighs to be signs of empathy, VD nodded grimly. Mahir's nails were digging into his palms. 'No way. This is not happening,' he breathed, his heart hammering. He would NOT sit through this. Beside him, Siddharth had gone completely still.

'Ananya was always fond of writing, and what better way to honour her than have a classmate write something for her . . . On this note, Yadav would like to read us a small poem he wrote for Ananya.'

A short, timid-looking boy hurried up to the front. Mahir didn't know who he was but he was sure as hell that he had no connection to Ananya.

'Life is fleeting . . .' the boy began reciting, his voice quivering.

'Stop,' Mahir's voice trembled as he whispered. 'Siddharth, make him stop.' What was going on? Was *this* their way of honouring Ananya's memory—asking a random student to recite some crappy poem for her?

'May I now request one of Ananya's classmates to share a few memories?' VD dabbed at her eyes, apparently touched by that ridiculous poem.

Mahir looked up. At least now they would call Veera or Siddharth to talk about Ananya. He knew that he would never be called to speak about her, no matter how much he wished he could.

His forehead creased as he saw a girl from Ananya's class getting ready to speak. She had a bored expression on her face.

'Ananya was a great friend. She always helped those in need. I can't remember a single time she was rude, swore or got angry. She was so intelligent . . .' The girl read from a piece of paper as though it was an infomercial and Ananya was the product she was trying to sell. Mahir would have laughed if he wasn't so infuriated.

He couldn't believe his ears. He didn't know whether to laugh or yell. He wanted to break something.

Siddharth squeezed his arm. He himself was rigid, his muscles tense.

'Her goodness and kind heart will always inspire us . . .' the girl droned on.

Mahir couldn't take it any more. He was suddenly on his feet, though he didn't remember getting up.

'This is bullshit,' he said, his voice echoing through the hall. And the entire school turned to stare. He could feel Siddharth tugging at his arm, begging him to sit down.

'Is there something you wish to share?' VD's voice was steely calm. Even without a mic her voice boomed.

Oh, he was in so much trouble now. But he couldn't care less. 'You know what? Yes. Yes, I do have something to share.'

He pushed his chair away noisily and walked down the aisle. Grabbing the mic from the girl, he growled, 'Go back to your seat.' The girl squeaked and scurried back to her place.

'This,' he gestured at everyone around, 'is bullshit.'

'Master Mahir Shah, I will not entertain—'

But Mahir cut her short. 'She died. She died, and now you hold a *prayer meeting* for her and ask some people who didn't know her from Adam to speak about her? Yes, she died. But I will not have you stereotyping her into your messed-up idea of "perfect" just because she's not here any more. That's not who she was.' His voice cracked.

He took a deep breath to stop himself from shaking. 'Just so you know,' he turned to the students, who stared at him, dumbstruck, 'Ananya was perpetually rude, she was a monster when she was angry and she swore *all the damn time*. But that didn't make her any less amazing. You want to talk about Ananya? Then talk about how fiercely protective of her friends she was, how she was always the first to apologize after a fight, how pissed off she got when someone messed up her coffee, or how she disappeared into the stories she read. You want to talk about her, then talk about the *real* her.' He glared at the crowd.

'Just because she's not here, doesn't give you the right to mar her memory for the rest of us and portray her as a completely different person.' He turned to the rest of the assembly. 'How are y'all standing for this nonsense?'

Silence.

Then slowly, a clap could be heard from the back, which was picked up by a few others, and so on, till the whole hall reverberated with thunderous applause.

Mahir stared at the dimwits in front of him. They were cheering. *Cheering*. Didn't they understand anything he had said?

'I am insulting you, you idiots!' he bellowed. 'Stop applauding!' Flipping the mic off, he threw it to a teacher, who caught it with a yelp. He stormed off, deciding he wasn't going to spend another second in this room full of idiots. To hell with the consequences!

He was almost at the door when a voice stopped him.

'You seem to know her awfully well.'

He cringed. He knew that voice well. Sunayana was one of the most popular girls in school, but to him she was only the fakest girl to walk this earth. He had once dated her—it had lasted a week.

He was surprised that he felt so much better after his dramatic speech, but he had forgotten that his batch didn't know he and Ananya had been close. It wasn't as if they had tried to hide it . . . It was just that as they grew up, their friend circles had diverged and they'd found themselves in the company of completely different people. But he confided everything in her. She was his go-to person, the one who was always there for him, no matter what his mistakes were.

In school, though, they were just polite with each other. Neither would leave their group to talk to the other. If it wasn't for Siddharth and Mahir's friendship, Ananya and Mahir would barely run into each other in school at all.

'And that's a problem because . . .?' he asked coldly.

She smirked. 'We didn't know you guys had been close.'

Mahir was very aware of everyone's gaze. Even the teachers had given up trying to regain any semblance of decorum. He swallowed. Should he admit that he and Ananya had been close for a long time? Why was he hesitating so much? Was he ashamed of her? No! But . . . but . . . Mahir Shah, the 'bad boy' of the school, close to Ananya Krishnan, a regular girl? A regular girl who wasn't his romantic conquest? That wouldn't really go with his reputation. For the school, Mahir Shah was a player; he wasn't 'just friends' with any girl.

So it finally comes down to choosing between Ananya and my reputation . . . Why the hell is everything so complicated?

And in that moment, he hesitated. And he hated himself for it but he couldn't unthinkingly pick Ananya.

'I . . .' he faltered. He caught Siddharth looking at him and saw his eyes darken with disappointment as he stammered through his indecision.

'I'm afraid that what Ananya is to him is none of your concern.'

Mahir's eyebrows shot up in wonder when he saw who had spoken.

Aakash.

His face blank, his voice steely, he stood looking at Sunayana with disbelief and disgust.

Out of the corner of his eye, Mahir saw Veera's hands fly to her mouth, and his heart went out to her. It must be killing her to see her best friend's death being used to fuel pointless drama.

Sunayana looked embarrassed. She couldn't win an argument against Aakash. He was too smart—and too involved with Ananya—for her to mock him. 'Aakash, I don't blame you—'

'So I suggest you sit down,' he spoke calmly, cutting her off, 'before you embarrass yourself further.'

Her face flaming, she threw a last dirty look at Mahir and sank into her seat in silence. Her look only aggravated Mahir. He was still seething. All the rage he'd suppressed since Ananya's death had come rushing back, blinding him. He needed to get out of here, to cool off, maybe hit something to release all the anger.

He turned and stalked out of the hall, slamming the door behind him. He heard footsteps following him but refused to look back. He broke into a run, which soon turned into a sprint.

Finally he reached the school ground, and since he was too spent, he stopped. The person behind him stopped as well, breathing heavily. Mahir turned.

'Two seconds more and I would've collapsed,' Aakash wheezed, holding his stomach in pain. He had never been the most athletic.

'What do you want?' Mahir growled.

'I think you meant to say "thank you",' Aakash replied.

'I didn't.' Anger sparked in Mahir's eyes. He tried very hard to be grateful to Aakash, but looking at him, all he felt was anger. Truckloads of it. 'Every time I look at you, I remember what you did to Ananya.'

Even as he watched, a glazed expression took over Aakash's face. Gone was the clarity that had been in his eyes just moments ago. The broken self had returned.

'Don't,' Aakash said quietly. 'Don't go there.'

'Why?' Mahir stepped closer. 'Is the great Aakash Acharya afraid to face his own past? Can he not own up to the fact that he broke Ananya's heart?'

'STOP!' Aakash yelled, losing his composure. 'You don't know what you're talking about. Don't speak until you know all the facts!'

'Facts!' Mahir scoffed. 'That's all it is with you. Facts and logic. And the one time that you listen to your heart . . . you mess even that up! You broke her.'

'No, *you* broke her,' Aakash snapped. 'You broke her heart and then you broke *her*.'

'What?' Mahir staggered, stunned. For the first time it struck him that maybe Aakash had felt slightly threatened by Mahir.

'You broke her with your actions. All she did was give you chances and all you ever did was let her down!' Aakash yelled. 'Even now, in the hall, you couldn't bring yourself to admit that you two had been close! She used to tell me about you and I could never see what she saw in you. Before we were together, all I wanted was for her to feel about me the way she felt about you. She believed in you for God knows what reason. And now I can't figure out why I ever wanted to be like you in her eyes. All you did was let her down.'

'Then why did you defend me?' Mahir asked, trying not to show how much Aakash's words affected him.

'I did it for her.' Again, Aakash's voice cracked. 'It's what Ananya would've wanted.'

'Now that she's not there, you do what "she wanted",' Mahir snorted. 'You played her, Aakash.'

Aakash's fist rammed into his nose. Mahir reeled backwards, completely winded, his head throbbing, and he could feel a trickle of blood snaking its way down his nose.

'You used her. You took her for granted,' Aakash spat and turned around. In a second, Mahir jumped on Aakash's back, pulling him down with him.

And they were locked in a fight. Mahir was more experienced, but Aakash's anger fuelled his punches. They rolled on the ground, punching and kicking, each trying to catch the other where it would hurt most.

Suddenly, Aakash scrambled up and, sliding his foot along the ground, kicked a spray of sand into Mahir's eyes.

Mahir cried out loudly. Holding up his hands, he yelled, 'Hey, man, that isn't fair! You can't throw sand into my eyes!'

'All is fair in love and war,' Aakash panted, wiping his mouth.

'Your punches suck.' Mahir got up, rubbing his eyes.

'Oh yeah? Well you suck,' Aakash shot back lamely.

They stood facing each other, dust swirling between them in the late-morning sunlight. They were both panting heavily, sweat streaming down their faces. Mahir had a bruised nose and his shoulders ached, while Aakash had a cut lip and a twisted ankle.

Without warning, Mahir's lips broke into a smile. Before long, he was howling with laughter on the ground as Aakash looked on, an amused smile making an appearance on his face. His first genuine smile in a long time.

'That felt good,' Mahir said. With all that anger gone, he finally felt like he could breathe again.

'For your information, that was my first fist fight.' Aakash offered Mahir his hand, which Mahir took gratefully to pull himself up.

'No wonder you sucked,' Mahir smirked. 'Okay, fine, not bad for a rookie,' he conceded.

'We are in so much trouble with VD, man,' Aakash suddenly said. But he wasn't exactly feeling remorseful. He couldn't remember the last time he'd felt this light. Fighting with Mahir had released the accumulating frustration.

Mahir started to laugh again. 'Oh, right, Aakash Acharya has never been in trouble before.'

Aakash raised his eyebrows. 'Is pretty boy jealous?'

Mahir fake-gasped. 'You think I'm pretty? That's *adorable!*'

Aakash rolled his eyes. 'Come, you'll be surprised how much influence I have with VD . . . being the "good boy" and whatnot.'

'You *were* a "good boy". Not any more, though. Good boys don't fight.' Mahir shook his head in mock disappointment.

Aakash smacked his head playfully and then held out his hand. 'We cool?'

Mahir shook it firmly. 'Definitely. You have more guts than I thought you did . . . I can see why Ananya liked you.' He looked at Aakash closely and saw a flicker of pain shroud his eyes. But it was gone in a moment.

Mahir exhaled. That pain had been too genuine. Maybe there *was* more to the Ananya-Aakash story than he knew.

'There's a lot you don't know yet. Stick with me and you might learn more,' Aakash stated, as though reading his mind. He started walking towards the principal's office, already thinking of ways to get off without too much punishment.

Mahir shook his head in amusement and followed him.

Aakash Acharya had surprised him, and Mahir Shah was rarely surprised.

Aslesha

Aslesha was halfway through sending a text to Ananya before she even realized what she was doing.

She stared at the phone in her hand, suddenly terrified of the pain that was inevitable once her brain comprehended her action. She still hadn't come to terms with the fact that there was no Ananya. How could she, when evidence of her existence lay scattered everywhere? Her messages, her pictures, clothes (that Aslesha had borrowed but forgotten to return) . . . she was *everywhere*.

Aslesha had always envied Veera and Ananya's friendship. The whole school knew them as one entity. There was no Veera without Ananya.

Aslesha craved such a friendship. Kavya was supposed to be her best friend, but Kavya wasn't exclusive. She wasn't Aslesha's best friend alone, she was also half the grade's best friend. Veera and Ananya were so evidently each other's, it was amazing. They were each other's number-one priority. It was a given that whatever Ananya knew, Veera knew too, and vice versa. They planned their lives around each other—classes, tuitions, everything. At parties, they entered together and left together. They were each other's plus-one at every event.

When Kavya didn't really seem to want that sort of friendship, Aslesha had turned to Siddharth. But even Siddharth was too social to be labelled her person. He especially got super touchy when Aslesha commented about him never having time for them.

Everyone searched for fairy-tale romances . . . Aslesha searched for fairy-tale friendships.

As she stared down at the envelope in her hand, guilt gnawed at her insides. It was just before midnight and Aslesha still hadn't got out of the habit of checking her phone for late-night texts from Ananya.

It had been an almost nightly ritual. They were both late sleepers and they would play endless quiz games and chat till the wee hours, until one of them felt sleepy enough to say bye. They had played so many games that she doubted if anyone could compete with them in Harry Potter trivia any more.

Guilt. So much guilt.

If she could go back in time and not do that one thing. That one thing that withdrew Ananya's trust from her forever. She couldn't even think of it without cringing.

She swallowed forcefully, trying to still her pounding heart. She watched the minute hand of the clock tick lazily towards twelve. The analogue half read 11.58 p.m.

It was 11.58 p.m. on 31 December. New Year's Eve. And in two more minutes, it would be a new year.

Pressing her hand against her temple, she glanced fearfully at the letter in front of her once more. Ananya had written this letter a year back, on New Year's Day.

11.59 p.m.

She was on the verge of having a panic attack.

Every New Year's Eve, Ananya, Veera, Kavya and Aslesha would have a sleepover. Truckloads of junk food, romantic-comedy marathons, never-ending rounds of Truth or Dare . . . They began each year together and ended it together. After the clock struck midnight, and after answering all the messages on their phones, the girls would go out on to Veera's terrace with their blankets and pillows, and talk endlessly. When Veera and Kavya fell asleep, Ananya and Aslesha would still be up and chatting.

It was moments like these that made Aslesha feel special.

Another wave of sadness overwhelmed her.

It was on one such sleepover, though before New Year's Eve, that Aslesha had shattered the forming bond between herself and Ananya. It was reckless, something she did without thinking. If she was to justify herself, she would only be able to say that it wasn't meant to happen—it had been a mistake.

Looking back now, she couldn't think of a *single* good thing that could have come out of what she had done.

12 a.m.

With a little cry, Aslesha grabbed the letter. Her phone wasn't blowing up with messages tonight. She knew her friends were thinking the same thing she was—Ananya wasn't with them this year.

Her fingers shook as she teased the flap of the envelope open with her fingernail. The only source of light in the house was the nightlight in her room. Her parents were out for dinner—they had invited Aslesha but she had flat out refused.

The pale white sheet of paper slipped out on to Aslesha's hand. She opened it slowly, the rustle of the sheets echoing through the silent house. On any other day, being alone in the house as the clock struck twelve would have terrified Aslesha, but not today. You stop being afraid of ghosts when your reality scares you more.

Unconsciously, Aslesha smiled as her eyes swept over the page crammed with Ananya's handwriting. Ananya always wrote with pens that weren't waterproof. Aslesha had once asked her why, because the ink would smudge at the slightest contact with water and the writing would be impossible to read.

'It's easier to destroy that way,' Ananya had answered, laughing.

This might have been weird to other people but Aslesha had understood. Writing was Ananya's way of venting. Ananya wrote about her feelings, and many times she was terrified that people would read those pages accidentally. So she ensured she never used waterproof ink. And every once in a while when her own thoughts were too painful for her and she felt like she needed a fresh start, she would tear up all that she had written, dump it in water and watch as it washed the ink away completely, leaving behind a mass of blank, blue-tinged paper.

With a sigh, Aslesha sat down on her bed and began reading.

Hey stranger, do I know you?
I know your likes and dislikes, I know how you look, I know what clothes you wear, but do I really know YOU?

Or do I just know the version of you that you wish me to see?

I'm furious with you. You may have basically destroyed the one thing that meant the most to me, but you know what? More than anything, I feel sorry for you.

Do you realize what you do, Aslesha? You've become so used to being different with different people that you have lost yourself. When you aren't surrounded by people, who are you? Do people tell you who you are or do you tell them? Do YOU know who you are? You may have won many things with this attitude, but the minute you have to pull people down to make yourself happy, you have lost at life.

If you have to constantly lie and pretend to be someone you are not, according to the person you are with, is that person even worth being with? Isn't the whole point of friendship the fact that you are accepted for who you are?

The minute someone 'cooler' comes along, you dump the person you are with and move on.

What the fucking hell were you thinking? Did you like Aakash? Did I do something to piss you off? I can't think of one reason for why you would go against me like you did.

When I found out about what you had done, I was really angry. But then I realized that I'm not mad at you at all. I'm mad at myself. I'm angry that I thought I could trust you. I'm furious that I let you manipulate me into saying things that I never would have said, never would have even thought, at two in the morning, when I was at my most vulnerable.

You, Aslesha Narayan, have built ALL your friendships on a foundation of lies.

I've tried to tell you all of this in person. I've tried everything, from telling you light-heartedly to throwing it in your face that your attitude is not doing any of us any good. But you refuse to take the hint. I can't help someone who refuses to acknowledge their issues.

I've been telling you this since forever but you don't seem to understand. I am not your friend so that you can agree with everything I say. You are entitled to your own opinion. I didn't want a clone, I wanted a friend. A friend will tell you when you are wrong and tell you the ugly truth even if it hurts. They would rather hurt you with a truth than comfort you with a lie. They'll say what should be said and not what you want to hear.

A friend will not constantly agree with you to get on your good side. Nor will they look for personal gains in their relationship. All of us were friends with you for who you were, we didn't need you to change for us to love you. But you did, and that makes me feel like I have failed as a friend.

Honestly? I don't even want to see your face right now. But that's because I know I'll end up saying all of this to you. But what's the point? It'll make no difference to you. Have you gone one day without lying? One day without backtracking hurriedly when people don't agree with your opinion?

I'm disappointed. If I let you see what goes on in my head, I expect you to guard that knowledge with your heart and soul. Because that's what I would do for every one of you guys. I used to think that I was a good judge of character and I took pride in the fact that I chose my friends carefully. And man, I am pissed off at being proven wrong.

It's going to be a long time before I ever trust you again, and I can only hope this incident has taught you that without strength of character . . . we are nothing.

Ananya

Tears slid down her face as she stared at the letter, her heart thudding. That's it. It was the end of the page. A sudden surge of anger exploded in her head. How dare Ananya say these things? She was nothing like what Ananya had said. What happened was a mistake, there was no reason to analyse Aslesha's character and make such a big deal of it!

You refuse to take the hint.

Oh God. Aslesha buried her face in her hands. Was she actually justifying what she did? Maybe Ananya was right. She just couldn't take the hint. What if she was actually such a person? Could she be so horrible without even realizing it? Being different with different people was second nature to her. It made people like her. She preferred to think of it as part of her social skills rather than as some sort of character flaw. Regret made her nauseous. How was she supposed to find closure with Ananya now?

She stood up and walked to the mirror in her room. The same black, beady eyes, button nose and long, straight, dark hair that she knew so well—then why did she not recognize the person looking back at her?

Who *was* she?

Suddenly the cuckoo clock outside her room chimed, indicating that it was now 1 a.m. The sound startled her and she came out of her trance.

'This is bullshit,' she muttered, her forehead creasing. 'It's one in the morning. That's the reason I'm getting so emotional.'

She moved closer to the mirror, staring into her black eyes. The only way to put this behind her was to prove Ananya wrong.

She would show her that her friendships were not based on lies. School opened in two weeks' time. Ananya said that she couldn't go one day without lying?

We'll see about that.

Aakash

Being a good boy had its perks.

For instance, nobody questioned him when he asked to be excused from class because he had 'work'.

New Year's Day had been an absolute disaster. He had tried taking part in the festivities, but it wasn't long before he'd noticed that he was just bringing down everyone's mood. Some of his relatives had proposed a toast for Ananya so 'her soul may rest in peace', and that's when Aakash had had enough. He'd spent the rest of the day, and most of what remained of the holidays, shut up in his room and shutting people out.

Walking down the corridor now, he cringed at the hideous memory. He wished somebody would understand that Ananya was never meant to rest in peace. She was the sort of person who was meant to raise hell and change the world.

As he walked, his thoughts strayed to the final-exam schedule that had been posted on the noticeboard, but that was not what he was worried about. It was what came after the exams that made him uneasy.

Twelfth—the year that would supposedly decide their futures. The students knew that as soon as they entered Class XII, their workload would increase drastically, they would have to start building their résumés and applying to colleges. He shook his head as he realized that all condolences were so cursory. No matter what happened, life never stopped for anyone. A few months back, Aakash had been so stressed about all of this, but now—he couldn't care less. Those were things he'd worry about when he had to. As for now, being the perfectionist that he was, he was almost done with this year's portions for the finals, and sitting in class, doing the same thing again, felt too mundane.

Plus, he really did have something to do.

Looking around to see if anyone was around, he quickly climbed the stairs to the fifth floor—a large terrace where the school stored construction material and other bits and pieces. The terrace walls were very low and that was why it was out of bounds to students.

Silently, he made his way to the door and slid the bolt out of the lock, wincing as the clang echoed around him. In a practised manoeuvre, he pushed the door open an inch, squeezed through and immediately dropped to a crouch once inside. Since the parapet was low, anyone standing at the opposite end of the school building would be able to see Aakash if he stood up straight.

He could hear the dull pounding of his heart as he looked around the place. This was their place. Aakash and Ananya's. Their secret. They had spent countless hours here—talking about everything under the sun, and sometimes, just sitting silently, eyes closed, and basking in it. For Aakash, it was a memory of the time he'd spent with the girl he was beginning to really like.

Slowly, he made his way towards the far end of the terrace. There, behind the water tanks, was a tiny indentation, almost like an alcove. A tiny ledge jutting out on top protected it from the rain, but that's all. It was hidden from view but barely sheltered from the elements. Aakash hoped fervently that he would find what he was looking for. It had been about a year since he was on this terrace last.

His creased forehead smoothed as his eyes fell on what he had come there for. With a sigh of relief he reached his hand into the alcove and took out the single sheet of paper. Paper clutched in hand, he made his way back to the opposite end of the terrace and settled down with his back against the wall. This side of the terrace provided a great view of a part of the city, while keeping him hidden from prying eyes.

The sun beat down on him pleasantly as he closed his eyes for a moment, enjoying a rare moment of absolute calm. If he stayed like this, he could almost pretend that everything was normal.

He could almost imagine her presence at this spot—where they'd sat together so many times. He squeezed his eyes shut harder.

They were sitting side by side, when suddenly, a gigantic crow skimmed right over her head and landed inches from her. Ananya was terrified of crows. Out

of her mind with fear, she jumped on Aakash, yelling at him to shoo it away. While Ananya was cowering with fear, Aakash couldn't stop laughing.

'You do know that these guys are our ancestors, right?' Aakash chuckled, referring to the belief that their forefathers came to visit them in the form of crows.

'I couldn't care less, just make it go away!' She was hilariously hysterical.

Aakash managed to drive the crow away but Ananya refused to sit separately after that. She moved closer and leaned against him.

'You know, in case the crow comes back.' She shrugged when Aakash looked at her suspiciously. 'I'm sticking to you.'

She took out a textbook from her bag, even as he rolled his eyes, and began reading. He watched her for some time, wondering if she would do anything else. But when she didn't say anything, he dug out a book from his bag too.

They read in silence for a while, and Aakash was really getting into the world of organic chemistry, when he felt Ananya stir. She shut her book, yawned and stretched like a cat.

'I'm going to close my eyes for a bit,' she announced as she yawned again.

'Where are you going to sleep? On the ground?' He eyed the ground with distaste. It definitely wasn't clean.

Ananya rolled her eyes. 'No, idiot. This is where you make yourself useful.'

It took him a minute to understand. Before he could respond, Ananya was already putting his arm around her and snuggling to his side. Resting her head on his shoulder, she smiled up at him once, and then closed her eyes.

His heartbeat accelerated. He wondered if this felt as intimate to her as it did to him. He also realized that the arm he had around Ananya was still in the air. He had no idea what to do with it! Where should he keep it?

After a lot of thought, he let his arm encircle her torso, stiffening instantly, waiting for her to say something, but she didn't. He knew she wasn't asleep because her breathing was irregular. And a small, optimistic part of him *wondered if that was because of him. The realist in him, though, crushed that thought immediately.*

Ananya Krishnan drove him crazy without even trying. She made him want to jump off a building just to stop the riot of emotions he was feeling. But more than anything, he felt confused. Confused, because he didn't really understand why being with her made him feel this way and why it felt like such a big deal.

And yet now he sat alone, on the same terrace. If he squeezed his eyes shut hard enough, he could feel the sun that beat down on them that day. He could feel the pressure of Ananya's body next to him as she lay absolutely still. He could still feel the urge that he had felt that day to rest his head on hers and close his eyes too, but he hadn't been able to tear his eyes away from her face. The urge to brush away that stray strand of hair tickling her nose, causing her to sniff adorably. He loved the way the sunlight glinted off her wavy dark-brown hair. He loved how it made her coffee-brown eyes seem like molten gold edged with black when she finally stopped pretending to sleep and opened her eyes to talk. He loved how animated her expressions were. But most of all, he could feel the dull ache in his chest because he knew Ananya would never lie like that again.

It was the most clichéd story of all times. Had Aakash read his and Ananya's story in a book, he would have snorted and dismissed it, saying such things didn't happen in real life.

He knew Ananya would never feel about him the way he did about her. He was the nerd who got good grades, was boring and didn't have anything extraordinary to say about himself except that he was smart. All that smartness wasn't doing him any good now! And she was the type of girl who preferred the bad boys who would sweep her off her feet and take her on midnight adventures. Someone like Mahir. It was one of the reasons Aakash had always felt threatened by him. And Aakash? Man, he would probably be friend-zoned for all of eternity.

Now he wondered whether he preferred being friend-zoned but always close to Ananya, or being more than a friend but apart from her forever. It didn't matter one way or another.

'Brooding again, are we?'

Aakash's eyes flew open and he scrambled up. If he was caught here, he would be dead. So his features automatically relaxed when he saw Mahir's impish smile.

'I can't seem to get rid of you,' Aakash grumbled, but Mahir's grin only widened. 'How did you find me?'

'I followed you. It's really funny how you think you're being so cautious when you're really just so dumb,' Mahir said, sitting down. 'I didn't want you to throw yourself off the roof or something, so I came to check. If anyone gets to throw you off a roof, it's me.'

Aakash rolled his eyes.

'What's that?'

Aakash looked down at the piece of paper clutched in his hand. He bit back a curse. He really didn't want to open it in front of Mahir.

'Oh, you know . . . just a bit of spare paper.' Aakash slipped it into his trouser pocket.

Mahir chuckled loudly. 'Yeah right, now try the truth.'

Aakash sighed. There was no way he was getting out of this. Taking the piece of paper out again, he handed it to Mahir. 'This was Ananya's bucket list.'

Mahir frowned as he unfolded the shabby sheet. 'Dude, there are, like, three things on her list. Only three things . . .'

'Yeah, well, she didn't get the time to complete it . . . this was just the beginning.' Aakash grimaced.

'Ah.' Mahir nodded and dipped his head to read the list. 'Are you sure she wrote this?' he asked with an amused smile, holding up the list.

'Obviously, I was with her,' Aakash smiled. 'It's crazy, right?'

'Our handwriting is so similar!' Mahir remarked, ogling at the paper.

'That's my handwriting. She dictated, I wrote,' Aakash said. 'That means my handwriting and yours are similar.'

'Yeah,' Mahir said, not really listening any more. Aakash could see the gears turning in Mahir's head, undoubtedly thinking up something stupid.

'Mahir . . . are you fine?' asked Aakash, suddenly concerned. 'You look like you're having a seizure.'

'I'm fine, thanks.' Mahir rolled his eyes. 'But I have an idea.'

'No.' Aakash crossed his arms.

'But you haven't even heard my idea,' Mahir whined.

'It'll be something stupid, I'm sure,' Aakash replied. 'What? Don't look so hurt! Fine, tell me your dumb idea.'

Mahir whooped. 'Let's complete it. Ananya's bucket list!'

'How? I don't know what else she might have wanted to add, I mean it's *her* bucket—' Aakash started.

'Not the list, you smartass. I meant we complete the *bucket list*,' Mahir said dramatically.

Silence.

'Have you read the list?' Aakash asked.

Mahir nodded.

'Did you see the kind of things she wanted to do?' Aakash asked, exasperated.

Mahir nodded again.

'How the hell will we be able to do all that?' Aakash snapped.

'My idiot friend, for most people, the list is impossible. But when you're friends with *Mahir Shah*, nothing is impossible.' Mahir threw an arm around Aakash, smiling smugly.

'Wow, could you be any lamer?' Aakash deadpanned, though his heart was doing jumping jacks. Could they really do this? If they did, it would be fantastic. It would be like getting back a piece of Ananya.

'Shut up and say yes.' Mahir was practically jumping, which was *very* unlike him. 'I'll help you do all the things listed here.'

'Wait, hold on a sec,' Aakash said, frowning. 'If you're helping me do this, what do you want in return?'

'I'm doing this for free, I'm a generous guy,' Mahir smirked.

Aakash raised an eyebrow.

'No, wait, who am I kidding? I'm selfish as hell!' Mahir laughed. 'Of course I want something.'

Aakash's heart plummeted. He could always say no, but he was too taken by the idea now to back out.

'What do you want?' he asked with a resigned sigh. 'Ask for anything; except, I will not cheat, I will not steal, I won't break anyone's heart nor will I publicly humiliate someone.'

'Wow, wow.' Mahir raised an eyebrow. 'The return of the good boy.'

'Oh my God, will you just state your terms?' Aakash slapped his forehead in irritation.

'Okay, okay.' Mahir held up his hands in surrender. 'For every item that we cross off the list, you have to tell me a story about Ananya and you. Deal?'

Aakash would have been less surprised if Mahir had ordered him to kill someone. He nodded, slightly dazed.

'Yeah, fine, sure,' he stuttered. 'Why the sudden interest?'

Mahir shrugged. 'It's a part of her life I know nothing about.'

Aakash nodded, crouching as he made his way to the door. 'You really have to help me if we are to complete that list.'

Aakash watched Mahir carefully as he glanced down at the crumpled paper. Mahir handed it back to him, his eyes wide with surprise once more. Ananya's list would throw anyone off! And Aakash couldn't help smiling slightly as he glanced at the list again.

Ananya's Bucket List:
- *Be a badass and play a giant prank on the whole school*
- *Crash a wedding*
- *Fail a test (just to see the teacher's reaction)*

He looked up to see Mahir smirking. 'Don't worry,' Mahir said, 'this is gonna be ridiculously fun.'

Mahir

'Aakash, seriously, come out!' Mahir said, banging on the cubicle door. His face was red from holding in his laughter. 'It's time to be badass.'

A week after Mahir and Aakash had made their pact, Mahir decided that it was time to put the plan into action. Today, they would complete the first entry in Ananya's bucket list.

'You know, when I said I wanted your help,' Aakash's muffled voice came from behind the door, 'I didn't exactly mean, help to ruin my life. Isn't this a little extreme?'

'If you're going to be a bad boy, then I have to insist that you do it right! Opportunities like this don't come along every day!' Mahir sighed. 'Plus, you did promise to do as I said.'

A few minutes of grumbling later, Aakash opened the door with a scowl. 'Fine. Let's just get this over with.'

Mahir whooped happily. 'Let's get out of here.'

From the minute they stepped out of the bathroom, it was evident that Aakash was everybody's centre of attention. Mahir had to drag him to keep him from bolting back to the bathroom.

'What?' Aakash snapped at a couple of thirteen-year-olds who were staring at him wide-eyed. They scurried away at

Aakash's glare. Mahir smirked and continued leading him towards the Class-XI corridor.

'Okay, I've changed my mind. I'm not going inside!' Aakash yelped. Mahir rolled his eyes and, paying no heed to Aakash's whining, dragged him inside XI C.

The bell hadn't rung yet, so students from other sections were present too, lounging on chairs, laughing, playing pranks. As soon as Aakash and Mahir walked in, all heads swivelled to face them and an unearthly hush spread through the class, punctuated by a few dramatic gasps.

'Oh my God . . . Aakash?' Aslesha gasped, and poor Aakash looked like a deer caught in the headlights.

Veera was next. 'Your hair! It's . . . it's . . .'

'Blue!' Siddharth gasped. 'Dude, why is your hair electric blue?'

'It's not *completely* blue!' Aakash said defensively, slowly turning red. 'It's just one streak! Come on! It's not that bad!'

'I like it! It's so . . . badass,' Nikhil said, his eyes shining. 'Is it permanent?'

'No way!' Aakash said, shooting Mahir a glance. 'It's for something Mahir and I are working on.'

Everyone's attention suddenly shifted to Mahir. 'Boys, girls and fellow cranky teenagers,' Mahir began, not at all fazed by the attention. 'I present to you—Badass Aakash!'

'Badass Aakash? Yeah, right,' Kavya said, walking into the class. Then she caught sight of Aakash. 'What the hell? Aakash, your hair's blue!'

'Really?' Aakash shot his group a dry smile. 'I hadn't noticed.'

'Today, my fellow classmates, is going to be a day you'll never forget. Get ready to see a side of Aakash Acharya you've never seen!' Mahir announced dramatically.

'Okay, he's exaggerating! You can all go back to doing your work now!' Aakash said, slapping Mahir on the shoulder.

'I'm not exaggerating at all!' Mahir took Aakash's arm. 'Okay, we have to rush. Let the mayhem begin!'

And with a loud, evil guffaw, Mahir dragged Aakash out of the room.

'We're going to die,' Aakash wailed. 'I'll never score well in my boards, I'll never get into college, I'll never make my parents prou—'

'Will you shut up already?' Mahir whispered, as they crouched in a dark corner of the school office.

'We are breaking school rules!' Aakash whispered back.

'Only if we get caught,' Mahir answered. 'Besides, today is all about rebelling, right?'

'Can't we rebel within the limits of the school regulations?' Aakash whined.

'"Within the limits of the school regulations,"' Mahir laughed, mimicking him in a nasal tone. 'Shut up. Now repeat the instructions I gave you.'

'You know, you're just a big bully,' Aakash grumbled. 'Our "mission" is to get to that room with the controls to the PA system and the school bell. You will distract the staff, while

I run into the room—wait, remind me again why I have to run into that room?'

Mahir rolled his eyes. 'Because *you* are the one completing Ananya's bucket list, idiot. I'm just helping you out. Therefore, *you* put yourself under more risk, not me.'

Then, without warning, Mahir dashed out of their hiding place. He looked back once and saw Aakash taking deep breaths to calm himself, and for a second, Mahir was worried. Did Mr Golden Boy actually have the balls to see this through?

Right then, Aakash looked at Mahir, and when Mahir saw the resolve in his eyes, he was convinced. Aakash would do this for Ananya.

Mahir made a great show of wobbling to the front of the office. When he was in position, he let out a high-pitched scream and collapsed to the floor. The entire office turned to look at him.

'Aahhh! I'm hurt—ow!' he yelped. He cracked one eye open and saw Aakash slip into the room that had all the electrical mains. Now Aakash just had to find the switch for the bell. Mahir could see him frantically running around, reading labels, and he cursed. They were losing time.

'I asked you where you're hurt?' Mahir found a staff member kneeling down next to him.

'Oh . . . um . . .' Mahir had momentarily forgotten his act. He let out another cry of pain. 'Oh God! Ouch . . . my . . . my . . .'

'Back?' the teacher asked.

'No, my . . . my—ow!'

'Leg?' someone else supplied.

'Head?'

'Chest?'

'NO!' Mahir shouted, and everybody jumped. 'My . . . everything! Everything hurts! But mostly it's my heart! It hurts!' What the hell was he saying? Aakash should have been done by now. He was completely improvising and was clearly terrible at it.

'Heart? As in cardiac arrest?' All eyes widened in horror.

Mahir struggled to keep a straight face. 'No! it's a . . . it's a—' He suddenly went really still and dropped to the ground. He had to fight a smile when he heard the gasps all around.

'Oh my God, he's fainted! Someone call the nurse!'

'Should we call the principal?'

'No, no, no!' a teacher whispered loudly. 'Do you really want to explain to Ms Deshmukh how this happened on our watch?' Everyone agreed. Mahir mentally thanked God. If VD got involved, things would be a lot more complicated.

'Where is the nurse? Can someone give me a bottle of water?' Finally someone had taken charge of the situation.

He heard people moving around and suddenly he felt drops of water on his face. He barely managed to keep himself from flinching. A few seconds later, more water was sprinkled. And then some more.

Mahir could tell by the hushed murmurs that the staff was starting to get suspicious. He didn't have much time now. Why wasn't Aakash ringing the damn bell!

'I really think we should call Ms Deshmukh.'

'Not yet. Where is the nurse? She is never where she should be!' the same woman who had asked for the water bottle exclaimed.

'Here I am! Okay, okay—tell me what happened?' Shit! Mahir recognized the voice of the nurse. She listened as the teachers told her what had happened.

'First of all, I suggest you all back off a bit, so there's some fresh air,' the nurse said in a self-important tone. 'I think I need to take him up to my room. He must be dehydrated.'

There were murmurs of approval. Mahir was panicking. Aakash should have done his job by now! Mahir knew that he could buy a few more seconds if he dramatically recovered from his fainting spell, but after that there was nothing more he could do.

He felt someone grasp his legs and shoulders and try to haul him up. Okay, time was up.

With a jolt he shook himself and started coughing violently, startling everyone around him.

'What . . . what happened?' he asked, pretending to be dazed.

'You fainted,' the nurse said, as everyone around relaxed visibly. 'Now come on, I'll give you some Electral.'

'There's no need, I feel fine now. Thank you,' Mahir said, getting to his feet slowly.

'I'm not giving you a choice.' The nurse rolled her eyes. 'Back to work, you guys. It's all right, he isn't dead!'

The office staff turned to go back to their work.

'Thank you for your help!' Mahir said, trying to keep their attention.

They looked back at him and nodded, smiling.

'I don't know what would have happened if you hadn't been around!' Mahir insisted. Where the hell was Aakash?

The staff waved the gratitude away and smiled again, a little impatient now.

There was silence for a second as they turned, almost.

Then suddenly: Trrrrrrrrrrrrriiiiiiiiiinnnnnnnnnnnnnnnnnngggggggggg! Trrrrrrrrrrrrrrrrrrrrriiiiiiiiiiiiiiiiiiiiiiiiiiiiinnnnnnnnnnnnnnnnnnnng! Trriiiiiiiiiiiiiiiiiiiiinnnnnnnnnnnnnnngggggg!

Everyone looked at each other, thoroughly confused.

'That's three consecutive bells!' one shouted.

'FIRE!' the nurse screamed. 'EVERYBODY, OUT NOW!'

As everybody turned and ran helter-skelter without so much as a passing glance at Mahir, who had blended into the shadows. He managed to slip into the room.

'What the hell took you so long?' Mahir yelled. 'There I was, saying absolute rubbish while YOU . . . Aakash? Aakash? Are you listening to me?'

Aakash was staring open-mouthed at the screens all around him that showed different parts of the school. Students were swarming out in one big human wave as the teachers herded them like cattle. They walked dully down the stairs to assemble at the playground. As far as they were concerned, it was just another boring mock drill.

'I did that!' Aakash whispered, and burst out laughing.

'Uh . . . Aakash?' Mahir stared at him, bemused. 'This is really not a good time to go psycho.'

'This is the most fun I've had in ages! The thrill . . . it's almost like being with Ananya again!' For the first time since her death, Mahir noticed that Aakash had spoken about her happily.

He smiled. No smirk this time, no sarcasm. He smiled a genuine smile.

'You haven't seen anything yet.' Mahir whipped out a recorder. He switched on the PA system (a speaker attached to a tree in the grounds made outdoor announcements possible) and, holding the recorder close to the mic, pressed play.

'Fire is catching,' Jennifer Lawrence's voice as Katniss Everdeen echoed through the entire school. Aakash was rolling on the floor, silently laughing as he saw the screen that showed the school ground. The teachers were running around, trying to stop the students from moving too much, while simultaneously trying to figure out if there really was a fire. But the moment the speaker crackled to life and the recording played, every single one of them froze, unable to comprehend this bizarre situation.

'And if we burn, YOU BURN WITH US!' Mahir paused the audio, noting the expression of recognition dawn on the students' faces.

After a second's pause, he pressed play again, and this time a remixed version of 'Fire Burning' by Sean Kingston blasted through the speakers. Before Mahir could caution him, Aakash grabbed the mic and yelled, 'PARTYYY!'

And as the music blasted through the speakers, the students and teachers finally realized that they'd been pranked. The students immediately cheered, some even breaking into dance. The teachers were furious.

'Let's get outta here,' Mahir whispered. 'We have to be seen on the grounds so that they think it's not us.'

'Thank God, VD's not in today!' Aakash was grinning like a Cheshire cat, and Mahir chuckled at his manic enthusiasm.

Quietly they made their way downstairs and joined the rest of the school, currently in a state of absolute confusion. Mahir looked around, proud that he was the one who'd caused this. He saw teachers agitatedly trying to calm the younger children, and department heads threatening the older ones into confessing what they knew. But no one knew anything, and that frustrated the teachers even more. Although, it took the entire eleventh grade only a second to realize who the culprits were, when they saw Mahir and Aakash slip into the crowd.

Siddharth tackled the two of them in a giant hug when they were close enough. 'I'm really starting to like the blue streak,' he laughed. Nikhil couldn't stop rapping along with the song that was still playing, and Veera, Aslesha and Kavya were laughing their hearts out.

Mahir felt a surge of happiness.

For the next couple of hours Mahir and the rest of the school chilled out in the grounds. He watched as it took the teachers half the day to restore decorum. First, they checked for any possible fire threats. After that, when they were finally allowed into the school, the teachers tried to conduct an inquiry to find the culprit. But there were more than a thousand students in the school, and every single one of them was too excited, so the faculty soon abandoned their search.

Finally, their class teacher, Ms Tanvi, walked into XI C, and silence was restored within seconds.

'What happened today was unfortunate,' she began in a tired voice. Mahir and Aakash snickered. 'But,' she said, glaring at them, 'our test on the circulatory system will still take place irrespective of that. You have ten minutes to complete these objective questions, and they will be corrected and handed back to you before the end of this period. May I remind you all once again that tests are not to be taken lightly, and I sure do hope that everyone has prepared well.'

As she started handing out the question papers, Mahir heard Aakash next to him. 'I completely forgot about this!'

Mahir's eyebrows shot up and his eyes lit up as he turned to Aakash.

'No, forget it.' Aakash crossed his hands, the blue in his hair making him look comical. 'I'm *not* failing on purpose. If I hadn't been so busy being talked into this nonsense by you, getting my hair streaked blue, I might actually have studied for the test.'

Mahir shrugged. 'Fine, whatever.'

Ten minutes went by in a flash and, before too long, the teacher was asking for the papers to be passed to the front.

'How did you do?' Mahir asked, as he turned to take the paper from Aakash to pass ahead.

'Good, actually . . . I remembered her teaching this chapter, since, you know, I *do* pay attention in class.' Aakash cracked his knuckles and chuckled as Mahir rolled his eyes and turned his back to him.

'I forgot to write my name!' Mahir said suddenly, grabbing a pencil and scribbling his name. He then passed the papers ahead.

As the teacher started correcting the papers, Mahir saw Aakash watching her expressions. His paper was somewhere in the top half. He knew that because Mahir and Aakash were sitting on the first bench in the last row of the class. She picked up another answer sheet. As she corrected it, her face became more and more confused. She reached the end of the page and looked up to see the name of the student. Her eyes widened in surprise.

'Aakash?'

Aakash's forehead creased. 'Yes, miss?'

'Could you come here, please?'

Aakash stood up and went to see his test paper. When he did, his eyes nearly popped out of his head.

Mahir was quite close to the teacher's desk, so he caught snatches of their conversation.

'Failed . . . what do you mean, *failed*?'

'This is your paper, right?'

Aakash looked at the solved sheet and let out a sigh of frustration as he finally understood what had happened.

'There has been a mistake, ma'am,' Aakash said. 'I know all the answers . . .'

'I understand that things have been hard recently—not to mention chaotic. But I can't allow you to take the test again. Don't worry, though, your average is high enough, so this one bad score won't impact your grade. Just promise me you'll work harder,' she said, stern yet kind.

Aakash sighed. He mumbled a sincere apology and returned to his seat.

'So this funny thing happened,' Aakash said, sitting down beside Mahir. 'Somehow, my name was written on a test paper that had your handwriting.'

'Really?' Mahir asked, trying to act innocent, a small smile playing on his lips. 'Must've been a mistake. I told you our handwritings were similar.'

'So you wrote my name on your paper right before handing it over?' Aakash asked.

Mahir snorted. Aakash was insulting his intelligence. 'As if. I wrote your name on my test in the beginning. When we were submitting the test I just replaced your name with mine on your test. Guess I get full marks on this one.' Mahir grinned.

Against his wishes, Aakash was amused.

'So you get full marks *and* you check another item off the bucket list.'

Aakash shook his head, but he was smiling. 'Don't ever repeat that, though.'

'I wouldn't dare,' Mahir laughed as the bell rang, signalling the end of school.

Siddharth

Fourteenth February was the day of the devil.

Siddharth hated everything about it. The obligatory flaunting of one's relationship, the way it made single people feel inadequate—everything about Valentine's Day screamed evil. But most of all, he hated the memories this day brought back.

He had lost track of the number of times he had planned something elaborate for Kavya, hoping and hoping that she would reciprocate. But she was never affectionate, which made Siddharth feel like he was being clingy. It felt like Kavya was with him only to fulfil the social requirement of having a boyfriend, and because it was convenient. When they'd started dating, neither of them knew what being in a relationship entailed. And Siddharth felt like it had dragged on for so long only because neither had known how to end it. Their fights had got pettier and pettier, and it was almost like they would look for excuses to not spend time with each other. He knew that Kavya would never break up—she would rather remain in a directionless relationship than lose the social benefits that came with being in one. On Facebook—peppered with a thousand happy pictures of the two of them—their relationship had looked perfect; Kavya loved to show off. In person, though, he'd felt like the time she spent with him was only as long as it took to click the photos that would validate them as a couple on Facebook. Siddharth understood that it wasn't easy for her to show her feelings, but after a point he had begun to feel unloved.

This had continued until he was practically suffocating in his own relationship and so he'd decided to end it. He'd told Kavya that they could say it was mutual, but what he hadn't realized was that Kavya wouldn't take kindly to being dumped, even if they did say that it was 'mutual'.

'God, I hate this day,' Veera sighed as she fell into step beside him. They had just finished with the last class for the day and were walking towards the school gate. There was a sea of students around them, all buzzing excitedly and discussing their plans for the day. Many girls were clutching roses or chocolate bars, and the scene made Veera feel even more sour.

'That's probably because we are sad and lonely,' Siddharth answered dourly. Veera smacked his arm.

'Thank God school's over,' she said gratefully. 'Now I just want to go home and relax. My parents are out for the evening too! But I have to start studying from tomorrow—I have to finish the entire portion in this study leave.'

'Oh God, someone hide me!' Siddharth said in a panicked whisper as he saw Kavya coming towards them. He had *really* hoped to avoid her today.

'Oh good, I have to sort things out with her anyway. It's been a while, and I'm sure neither of us meant half the things we said the other day,' Veera smiled slightly and started walking a little faster.

'What! Are you crazy?' Siddharth yelled. 'There is no need to sort things out with her! Why are you doing this to yourself?'

Veera laughed. 'Shh, it'll be fine.'

'Hi, Kavya,' she started, as Siddharth stood awkwardly to the side, staring at his feet. 'I'm sorry about what happened that day, I really hate fighting—'

But before Veera could continue, Kavya cut her off.

'So she's your rebound girl, then?' she asked Siddharth, her tone icy. 'Should have known—you have no taste.'

'Excuse me?' Veera frowned. And Siddharth raised his eyebrows.

As far as he knew, Kavya hated fights too, and this was very unlike her. Was she jealous? But he and Veera had been friends long before Kavya had even entered his life! What had changed now?

'Who are you and what have you done with my friend Kavya?' Veera asked.

Kavya smirked.

'I mean, I get it. You don't want to be alone on Valentine's Day, and Veera is desperate enough for any guy,' Kavya continued, still addressing Siddharth. 'Seriously, Siddharth, I really thought you had better taste.'

'Why are you being such a bitch, Kavya?' Siddharth finally looked at her, his eyes smouldering. 'Just leave us alone.'

'You won't be saying that when you come running back to me.' She turned to Veera. 'You're just a pastime. The sooner you realize that, the better it'll be for you.' Then she spun on her heels and walked away before Veera could say anything.

'That bitch!' Veera yelled, lunging after her. 'Let me at her!'

'Wow, calm down!' Siddharth said, holding her back.

'When I catch her, I'm going to rip her hair from the roots and painfully break every one of her nails and—*what?*' Veera stared at Siddharth, who was shaking with laughter. 'WHAT?'

'It's just . . . you're cute when you're angry,' he said, finally letting her go.

'Oh . . . um.' Veera could feel her face heating up and that only made Siddharth laugh more. He didn't know why but everything Veera did these days seemed cute or adorable. Especially the way she handled compliments.

'But no, seriously . . . What's got into her these days? How can she talk to *anyone* like that?' Veera scrambled for a change of topic. 'She treats you like you're her . . . her *lapdog* or something.'

Siddharth shrugged but didn't interrupt as Veera continued her rant. They had reached the school gate.

'She can't just treat you like you're her property! Like she knows you best.' Veera stopped and looked at Siddharth. 'It *annoys* me.'

Siddharth stopped laughing, but the smile on his face remained. 'Wow, is Veera Vishwanathan getting possessive of me?' He usually got defensive when his friends got possessive, but strangely, this time it felt nice.

Veera rolled her eyes. 'You wish.'

Siddharth raised an eyebrow.

'Okay, fine, maybe!' Veera said dramatically. 'Why do you enjoy embarrassing me so much? Bye! I'm going now, before I say something even more stupid.'

She started walking away, but Siddharth reached out and tugged at her schoolbag. Veera stumbled backwards, right into Siddharth. He caught her shoulder to steady her as she awkwardly turned around to face him.

'Wow, smooth,' Veera said, rolling her eyes, although she noticed that they were standing too close for comfort.

Siddharth tilted his head and studied her—it was fun watching her squirm. He smiled lightly.

'You should be possessive more often, idiot,' he said, his voice barely a whisper. Then, just as suddenly, he grinned and stepped back, laughing as Veera coloured.

But Veera didn't seem to realize it and stayed frozen to the spot, staring up at him with wide eyes. He stared back at her with such intensity that neither had the courage to break eye contact.

What was he doing? This was Veera, his childhood friend. And he was flirting with her?

This riot of emotions, the constant need to tease her, to watch her fumble because of the things he said . . .

Where were these feelings coming from all of a sudden? Was it because he was no longer with Kavya? No longer afraid to feel them for someone else?

Suddenly, Veera stepped back, realizing she was free to go. Her eyes were clouded with confusion and she cleared her throat as though that might possibly clear her thoughts.

'Um, okay, bye.' She tried to smile, but even that came out shaky. She turned and ran to her car.

Siddharth watched as the car drove down the road. He swore as he ran his hand through his hair.

Veera

Veera slammed her car door shut and leaned back against the seat, inhaling deeply. As she drove away from the school, she couldn't bring herself to look back—she knew Siddharth would still be standing there. And she didn't trust her expression to remain neutral.

Siddharth and Veera had always been just friends. She remembered telling Ananya that Siddharth and she were like an old married couple. They always quarrelled over little things and called each other out on their bullshit all the time. If she looked fat in a dress, Siddharth would tell her. If she did something stupid, he would be the first to laugh. But at the same time, they were fiercely protective of each other and were the first to jump to the other's defence.

Her car pulled over at the entrance to her building's lobby. She sighed and stepped out, making her way to the lift. Pressing the button for the sixth floor, she waited.

She was so confused! Things had never been this way with Siddharth. Sure, they flirted lightly all the time, they got jealous easily and they looked out for each other, but this was different. Things had suddenly become intense. The dynamics of their friendship seemed to have changed—at least in her head.

Was it because he and Kavya were no longer together?

Could it actually be that Siddharth just wanted someone to be with right now, and she was just available, like she had always been for him? Was Kavya right?

Even before she completed the thought, she knew it was bullshit. Siddharth was not like that. He would never do that to her. Besides, if he really did need a rebound, there were a hundred other girls willing to be that for him.

The lift dinged open and she stepped out.

'You know what,' she muttered to herself as she fumbled in her bag for the house key, 'we've been spending a lot of time together—that's why you're thinking these dumb thoughts. Things have been a mess lately. They'll settle soon enough. You just have to not make any stupid decisions till then.'

Opening the front door, she walked in, chucked her bag on the floor and kicked off her shoes.

'Mom! I'm home!' she sang.

'In here, Veera,' her mom called from inside. 'I was just about to leave.'

'Oh right! Arjun's play! But isn't it too early?' she asked, leaning against the door.

'No, no. We have to be there an hour early. I know, I know, these things always start late. But even if the show starts at 7 p.m., they have some performance or the other *before* it begins,' her mom explained as she put on her earrings. 'Anyway, we'll be late, so order what you want for dinner. Are you sure you don't want to come?'

'Does Arjun want me to?' Veera asked, smiling.

Her mother rolled her eyes as she checked to see if the clasp was in place, and picked up her clutch. 'I don't think he cares who watches! He's just so excited about the show.'

Veera laughed. 'Then I'm staying home. I'm exhausted.'

Her mom continued. 'Dad and Paati are already in the car, I was just waiting for you to get back.' She walked around the house, picking up her phone and keys. She paused at the door. 'Bye, Vee. Be careful—lock the door, okay? And call if you need something.'

'Bye, Mom.' Veera waved as her mom shut the door behind her.

She glanced at the clock on the wall. It was 4.45 p.m. She had the whole house to herself, and money to order food. Maybe an evening of chilling out was what she needed.

She decided to shower quickly and nap for a while. Napping would also ensure that she didn't think about Siddharth for some time.

She grabbed a towel and disappeared into the bathroom, humming to herself.

Siddharth

Siddharth was standing at Veera's door, tense, because his finger had rung the bell before he could decide if he actually wanted to do this. There was no answer. Did she have any class today? He glanced at his watch—6 p.m. She should definitely be at home. He rang the doorbell again.

A second later she opened the door, dressed in harem pants and a loose top. Her hair was up in a casual bun and her face looked like she'd just washed it. Her eyes almost popped out of her head when she saw Siddharth standing there with a giant bag.

'Hi!' Siddharth grinned like it was the most normal thing in the world, but his insides were balled up with the fear of rejection. Of humiliation.

Veera squeaked and slammed the door shut.

Okaaayy . . . not what he had expected. Before he could ring the bell again, the door opened, but just a crack. He could see a large, brown eye staring at him.

'What are you doing here?' Veera hissed.

'Wow, nice to see you too,' Siddharth replied.

'Sorry, you know that's not what I meant,' Veera sighed. 'What do you want?'

'Let me in and I'll tell you.'

'I can't.' Veera's eyes widened, like she was panicking.

'Why?'

'I just can't.'

'Is there somebody else in the house?'

'No.'

'Are you harbouring a fugitive?'

'Oh, shut u—'

'Oh my God, do you have a *guy* over?' he asked suggestively, just to annoy her. There was no chance of that and Siddharth knew it.

'Don't be an ass—'

He could almost feel her blushing. 'Then I don't see why I can't come in.'

'You just can't.'

'Why?'

'Because . . . I'm in my *nightdress*,' she whispered like she was letting him in on the world's most closely guarded secret.

Siddharth stared at her eye. 'You cannot be serious.'

'You don't understand!' He heard her stamp her feet in frustration. 'I'm not *presentable* right now! My hair's a mess and I'm wearing some shitty, weird clothes and my face has nothing on it! I feel naked meeting people without eyeliner,' she stage-whispered.

Siddharth rolled his eyes. 'I couldn't care less,' he said, pushing the door open. 'And besides, it's not like I'm going to be checking you out, so calm down. Geez!'

Despite Veera's loud protests, he barged in, dumped his bag by the door and turned to face her. She was wearing a Tom-and-Jerry top and a very pissed-off expression.

'What happened to "I'm not going to be checking you out"?' Veera asked, raising her eyebrows.

'Tom and Jerry! Nice top,' he grinned, trying to hide the flush creeping up his neck.

'Now that you're in, tell me what you want,' Veera said, crossing her arms. Siddharth wanted to burst out laughing at how adorably angry she looked.

'Okay, so today's crappy Valentine's Day, plus you had that stupid fight—you know, altogether, it's been super fun,' Siddharth started. 'So I thought we could round it off with something even more fun. And I thought you could use some company.'

Oh God, could he sound any *lamer!* It had been an impulsive decision; he hadn't been able to think of anyone else he'd rather be spending today with—talking about how much Valentine's Day sucked, *of course.*

Veera stared at him, her gaze cryptic. 'But Kavya? We just had another fight and I don't think we should—wait, where are you going?'

Siddharth was walking out of the door. 'I'm going home. Kavya doesn't matter to me, okay? And I know for a fact that she doesn't matter to you either. You're just forcing yourself to feel remorse so you don't come across as a bad friend—'

'But—'

'Do you like to spend time with me, Veera?'

Veera bit her lip.

One of the first lessons that Siddharth had ever learnt was to not ask questions he didn't want the answers to. And yet, here he was, asking the stupidest, scariest question.

'Yes, a lot.'

Siddharth had no idea he had been holding his breath. 'The suspense was killing me.' He grinned. 'So do you still want me to go?'

'Technically, I never asked you to leave, actually,' Veera said, finally smiling. 'Get back in, loser.'

Siddharth smiled. 'Nice save.' He picked up his bag and walked into the house.

'So what's the plan?' Veera asked.

'We are going to do some major chilling,' Siddharth announced as he opened his bag and took out a handful of DVDs. 'Which one shall we watch first? I have *Transformers*, *The Spongebob Movie* and almost all the Bollywood hits in this disc. Oh, and I brought you some chick flicks . . . since, you know, you're a girl.'

'You brought me chick flicks?' Veera said, wiping an imaginary tear from her eye. 'That's the sweetest thing anyone's done for me.'

'Yeah, yeah, make fun of the nice guy.' Siddharth waved his hand dismissively. 'So? What's the verdict?'

'Do you have any horror in there?' Veera asked. 'I'm not in the mood to *feel* anything.'

'I don't know if you know this . . . but, um, you will *feel* scared,' Siddharth said sarcastically.

'Are you really that stupid, or do you just pretend to be?'

'Okay, pro tip: always be nice to the guy who brings you chick flicks,' Siddharth grinned as he rummaged around in his bag. 'What about . . . *The Conjuring*?'

'Perfect. Let's watch *Transformers* after.'

Veera led him to the kitchen and handed him a packet of instant popcorn. 'Here, make yourself useful. I'll get the room ready.'

Fifteen minutes later, they were lazing on the extendable sofa-cum-bed in the guest room, which doubled as a TV room, and had the best speakers and sound system (according to Veera). Half a dozen pillows were strewn around them, the AC was on full blast, and the lights were switched off. Veera held the remote in her hand, finger poised over the play button, while Siddharth sat ready with the popcorn.

'Fair warning,' Veera looked at Siddharth, 'you know that I absolutely cannot shut up during movies.'

'Just relax, will you?' Siddharth said, pulling her back so that her head was resting on the propped-up pillows. 'Stop being so conscious, this isn't the first time we've watched a movie together.'

She pressed play. And from the first minute, it was evident that neither of them was going to be scared.

'Oh my God, that girl is so unbelievably stupid! Why, just why, would you open that closet so late at night and when you're alone!' Veera was jumping off her seat. 'Aaah! I can't see this!'

She buried herself under the blanket as Siddharth howled with laughter. Suddenly, Veera's foot touched Siddharth's and he inhaled sharply.

'You're freezing!' he said.

'I wouldn't be if you could just give me the damn blanket! You're literally sitting on the entire thing.' Veera tugged at the blanket to get it out from under his leg as Siddharth watched her struggle.

'Get in here.' He ordered, lifting the blanket to cover both of them. 'You'll die of hypothermia otherwise.'

Veera did as she was told and gently slid in, trying not to touch Siddharth with her cold body. The warmth was instant and she settled down with a content sigh.

Close to the movie's end, Veera could barely sit still, the blanket askew again. She was frantically trying to not look at the screen and still look at the screen. She grabbed Siddharth's hand and covered her eyes with it, parting his fingers from time to time to peek at the movie.

'Why did I agree to watch this movie?' she almost shouted. 'Aah, the anticipation is killing me!'

'Veera!' There were tears in his eyes from laughing so hard. But she would not stop shaking. He paused the movie.

Turning to face her, he quickly put his hand on her mouth, but that just made her laugh harder. She tried to lick his palm to get him to pull back, but he pressed down harder, making it impossible to open her mouth. After a few minutes she stopped giggling, but he could feel her smiling under his palm.

'Are you calm now?' he asked. She wrinkled her nose in disdain and nodded. He let go of her immediately.

'Now get back under the blanket!'

He pressed play just as she slid into the blanket once more. But this time there was a weird tension in the air.

'Oh, what the hell,' he sighed and, putting his arm around her, pulled her closer. Unsteady, she put her hand on his chest to keep from falling on him, but ended up being crushed to him anyway.

He winced again as the cold from her palm seeped through his shirt, and Veera started moving away, an apology ready on her lips. But he pulled her back.

'Stay, please,' he whispered. His heart was thudding unnaturally hard. For a moment he thought that she would pull away, but instead, she just rearranged the blanket around them and settled back down, this time laying her head on his shoulder. A sigh escaped him, and he was glad that she was on his right; his heart, struggling to jump out of his body, would undoubtedly have thudded to her attention, had she been on his left.

Taking her frozen hand into his warm ones, he slipped his fingers through hers.

'It'll warm them,' he said, more to convince himself than her. She only squeezed his hand in response and closed her eyes.

'No, no, no!' Siddharth nudged her. 'The movie's almost over! Watch the ending.'

Veera shook her head, a small smile painting her lips. 'I don't like endings.'

'But endings are happy.'

'Not in my life,' she whispered, burying herself deeper into the crook of his neck.

He didn't really have an answer to that.

Veera

Veera became dully aware of her surroundings even though her eyes remained firmly shut. She couldn't hear the TV and wondered how long she had been asleep. She could smell the popcorn in the air and her stomach growled. Her nose was freezing—the only part of her body exposed to the AC. She was in no mood to get out of this pleasant, half-awake state she was in, but when she tried to turn to a more comfortable position, she realized she could barely move. Almost at the same moment she became aware of how warm she was, although it was hardly unpleasant.

Sighing, she opened her eyes—and found her face inches away from Siddharth's. She stifled a cry of surprise as she finally realized how they were lying. As slowly as she could, she felt around for her phone to check the time. 8.45 p.m. No wonder she was hungry. They'd been asleep for only fifteen minutes . . . strange . . . It felt longer.

She had no idea when they'd both dozed off and how in the world her legs had ended up between his. The blanket was wrapped securely over them and she was crushed to his chest, her face resting in the hollow of his neck and his chin resting on the top of her head. Gently, she drew her face back to stare up at the sleeping face of Siddharth Ahuja.

He looked so much younger as he slept; his forehead creased slightly, strands of hair falling into his eyes, and she wondered what was worrying him. Siddharth hated stressing others out. Veera was usually the only person he shared any of his problems with, and even with her, he would only casually drop hints. These past months she'd been so preoccupied with herself that she hadn't even considered how it must be for him. He had taken care of her and she had let him. She felt really guilty.

When she looked at him, she saw the boy who had been nothing but supportive of her. He'd always been there for her, had taken care of her these past months, and hadn't once been scared away by her meltdowns.

He was one of her *best friends*; they'd always been close— but why was this different? What was happening? She felt a little pathetic—how stupid was she, really? The moment a guy showed even the slightest interest in her, she had to immediately start thinking long-term. Maybe Kavya was right, maybe she really *was* that desperate for attention.

She grimaced. Attempting to put some distance between them, she tried twisting out of his grasp without waking him. But instead, she felt his grip on her tighten ever so slightly, and before she knew it, he had pulled her to him, his hand pressed to the small of her back.

As she strained to look at his face, her shirt rode up a little and she felt his hand on her skin. Thoughts and sensations ran riot.

What's happening? What's he doing to me and how is he making me feel this way?

Breathless, she glanced up at the boy responsible for her pounding heart and noticed with relief that his eyes were still closed. So this was just a reflex in his sleep? Is this how he had been with Kavya?

A spike of inexplicable anger pierced her gut at the thought of Kavya. At the thought of Kavya with Siddharth.

'I wish I knew what went on in that head of yours.' Veera jumped at Siddharth's voice. He hadn't moved an inch.

'Guess you'll never know,' Veera said, her tone harsher than she had intended it to be. It didn't go unnoticed.

'Hey.' He tilted her chin up and she realized, both relieved and disappointed, that his hand was no longer on her back. He was *always* doing things like that. Hugging her when she could do with a hug, just casually resting his chin on her head, or tilting her chin up when she didn't meet his eyes. He did it so easily, so effortlessly, like it didn't mean more than just a friendly gesture to him. How did he not realize that her pulse skyrocketed every time he held her?

'What's wrong?' he asked again, his tone resigned. She knew he was readying himself to make her feel better, and that annoyed her more.

What *was* wrong, really? She was just thinking painful, futile thoughts and ruining her own mood. Siddharth had done nothing but try and cheer her up. She took a deep breath, trying to still her rogue heart.

'Nothing—' she started, her voice slightly shaky, but was interrupted by the sound of the main door opening.

'Veera! Where are you?'

In a split second Veera had pushed Siddharth off the bed and scrambled up. The guest-room door was closed, so she had a minute at best before her mother came in to see . . . . *oh God!* She almost died of embarrassment as she visualized her mom coming in and seeing her *sleeping* in the *same bed* with a *boy.*

'Ow! What was—'

Veera launched herself at Siddharth, slapping a hand over his mouth to shut him up. He raised an eyebrow and she felt him smirk between her fingers.

'If you wanted me so badly, you could have just asked,' Siddharth mumbled under her hand and Veera went scarlet.

'Shut up,' she stuttered. She scanned the room quickly. Where the hell would she hide him? Her eyes landed on the bathroom door.

'I'm really sorry, but I'll make it up to you.' And without further explanation, she pushed him into the bathroom, slamming the door just as the handle of her door turned.

'Mom!' she said, running a hand through her hair. 'I thought you guys said you wouldn't be back until much later! Did Arjun's event end early?'

Veera's mom nodded, not even glancing around the room. 'One of Arjun's friend's fathers turned out to be an old schoolmate of Dad's! They invited us to dinner, and since we had time to spare, we thought, why not? I came here to grab a bottle of wine and check if you wanted to come along. Arjun and Dad are in the car.'

'Have you seen the state I'm in?' Veera said, opting for a chuckle that she hoped sounded convincing enough.

Luckily her mom laughed. 'Fine then, see you! Don't stay up too late, okay?' She walked out of the room, wine bottle in hand. A few minutes later Veera heard the front door shut. She exhaled. But her relief didn't last long.

The bathroom door banged open, scaring Veera half to death. Siddharth walked out, looking terrified.

'Those,' he said, 'were the scariest two minutes of my life.'

'Can you imagine if my mother had walked in on us . . . on us . . .'

'On us what, Veera?' Siddharth asked, amusement replacing his shock. Veera stared at him. Two seconds ago he'd been as terrified as she was, and the minute he saw her freaking out, he was grinning?

'Forget it,' she mumbled. A second later she giggled. She looked at Siddharth and giggled again.

'What is it?' asked Siddharth warily.

'This whole incident was so funny.' Veera burst into laughter. 'Admit it! It was hilarious! I shut you in my bathroom! Such Bollywood potential!'

'No, it wasn't funny.'

'It was a little funny.'

'Okay, maybe a little,' Siddharth chuckled, unable to keep a straight face.

Smiling, Veera turned to grab her phone. 'Oh my God, I have to tell Anan—' She stopped. For a moment she couldn't breathe.

And then grief punched her in the gut all over again. For a few days she had actually felt okay, and not the if-I-ignore-my-grief-enough-it-will-go-away okay. Things had felt normal. Now she couldn't look at Siddharth. She turned away as her face burned with embarrassment and her eyes became moist.

'It's okay,' Siddharth said softly.

'It's not,' Veera said, still not looking at him.

'It happens, it's fine.' He started moving towards her.

'Fine?' Veera snapped. 'I fucking *forgot* that my best friend was DEAD! How is that fine?'

How could she have been so stupid? What sort of person *forgot* that her best friend was dead? To think that until a few minutes ago she had actually been enjoying herself. Ananya would never do the things Veera had all her life to do. That thought pierced her like a knife.

She took a deep breath. 'Siddharth, I think you should go now.'

'What happened? You were okay just a few minutes ago,' Siddharth said, peering at her.

'I—I can't be this way,' Veera said, almost to herself. 'I can't have fun.'

'Why? Why do you keep doing this to yourself?' Siddharth sounded slightly irritated and that fanned her temper.

'Doing what?' she snapped.

'Purposely making yourself miserable? It's like you can't bear something good happening to you!' He was almost shouting. Veera's temper flared again. He had no right to be angry.

'What bullshit!' Veera retorted. 'You don't know me, so you can stop pretending like you do!'

'Oh, I do . . . I've known you—I don't know—since forever!' Siddharth ran a hand through his hair in exasperation.

'You don't let yourself go, Veera! You don't let yourself have fun!'

'You don't understand!' Veera yelled, her voice cracking. 'I'm not *supposed* to enjoy anything!' She felt a twinge of pleasure when she saw his stunned expression.

'I'm not allowed to enjoy my life when my best friend isn't here to share it with me,' she continued. 'I can't go out and have fun when all I can think about is how she'll never get to do that any more!'

Siddharth opened his mouth to interrupt, but Veera didn't give him a chance.

'Every time I laugh, I remember how she will never laugh again. How I'll never see her laugh again. Everything I do reminds me of her! I spent my seventeenth birthday alone and "miserable"—like you pointed out—because I realized that Ananya will never turn seventeen! She'll never blow out the candles on her cake again, she'll never get to visit all the places she wanted to visit, never graduate or go to college. She'll never get to be with the love of her life or have her first kiss or even get married and have a family. *We*'ll never go shopping for birthday dresses again, we'll never have sleepovers, I'll never be able to hear her voice again, we'll never talk or play or laugh or do *anything* together again. I'll never have my best friend again.' She struggled to keep her voice audible.

Silence.

She didn't know what she expected Siddharth to say. But what he did say threw her off completely.

'You, Veera Vishwanathan,' he took a sharp breath, 'are the biggest idiot ever.'

What the hell!

But he continued, before Veera could ask him to get out of her house.

'Do you think Ananya would have wanted this?' He gestured at her. 'Let's get one thing straight. Being happy doesn't in any way mean that you're forgetting Ananya, okay? In fact, Ananya would have wanted nothing more than for you to heal.'

She lowered her face so he couldn't see the tears in her eyes. 'It doesn't concern you; what I believe is up to me.'

'I'm your friend, Veera! Why is that so hard for you to accept? Why can't you open up to me?' His hands were in his hair again, and almost unconsciously, Veera's fingers twitched. She wanted to remove his hands from his hair before he actually tore it out.

'*Why do you care?*' her voice shook, but her words had enough force in them to make him look up. She refused to meet his eyes.

'Because . . .' He gritted his teeth. Silence weighed down on them like bricks.

She heard him swear under his breath. And with a last 'forget it' he was out of the door.

There, she had messed up this friendship too. He had tried and tried to cheer her up, but she was determined to be miserable. Not only that, she also made everybody around her miserable. It was better this way. It was better if he stayed away from her.

Then why did it sting so much that he hadn't answered her question? Why didn't he tell her why he cared? *Did he care at all?*

She fell back on her bed with a sigh. She hated him. She *hated* Siddharth. She hated how he could just walk into her life and make everything look less horrible. She hated how her mind felt at peace in his presence, how all the annoying voices in her head finally shut up. And she *hated* that he actually wanted, and tried his best, to understand her. She hated thinking about how Siddharth probably had a hundred other fun things to do than spend time with her.

She and Siddharth had been friends ever since Class V. When he had started dating Kavya, Veera was his wingman . . . or wingwoman. There had been just two people in the world Veera could blindly trust and whose side she would always be on. Ananya and Siddharth.

Siddharth was the one who always goaded her into doing things she would never have done otherwise. She remembered him always forcing her to acknowledge her feelings instead of hiding them in a dark corner, to be dealt with later (*cough*, never). And she liked to think that she was his security blanket, the one he could always talk to. Veera had never felt one speck of jealousy the entire time Siddharth and Kavya were together. Maybe because he'd made sure that he never sidelined his friendship with Veera. He had a hundred friends, was the good, smart, popular boy of their class and couldn't be confined or 'restricted'—she remembered bitterly—to one friend circle, but he managed to keep all his friendships intact. Anyone who could be friends with Mahir Shah deserved respect.

Mahir Shah.

Her lips twitched almost involuntarily. Siddharth had been convinced that Veera and Mahir were made for each other and had gone to great lengths to convince her of it. He'd even tried to set them up on numerous occasions, resulting only in embarrassing and mortifying situations for Veera.

It was the usual story with Mahir. He'd been friends with her once, had found more popular friends and they'd grown apart. That's it, done.

But Veera knew she was kidding herself. Mahir and she had unofficially been together for more than a year, at a time when 'dating' was not such a big deal. If the guy liked you and you liked him back, it was usually enough to be considered dating. The saddest part, though, was that she didn't get closure. They just drifted apart as they grew older. And since there had never been anything 'official' between them, there was nothing to break off. Right now, after a really long time, she had reached a point in her life where her heart didn't ache when she saw him. She wasn't upset that it had ended, and, like she'd tried explaining to Siddharth on numerous occasions, she didn't want to get back with him . . . it felt wrong somehow. The only thing that upset her was that the two of them had never got around to being friends again.

With a resigned sigh, Veera walked to her dressing table and pulled open her jewellery box. It's where she'd hidden her letter from Ananya. Taking the creamy envelope in her hand, she walked back and collapsed on her bed, staring at her name, cursive and blood-red. This was it. If she read it, there was no going back. This was the last thing Ananya would ever say to her. Did she want to do this?

With a snort of annoyance at her gloomy thoughts, Veera peeled open the envelope and pulled out the sheaf of papers. She could see Ananya's loopy handwriting through the thin paper.

Ananya's handwriting was a lot like her. From a distance it seemed perfect, beautiful, unachievable. But when you took a closer look, you would notice the not-so-neat details—the tiny inkblots, the scratched-out sentences . . . just like how she seemed perfect and unattainable from afar, but up close, she was one of the most gullible and vulnerable people you could ever know. Gullible, not stupid.

Taking a deep breath, Veera began to read.

I believe in soulmates.

In fact, I believe in multiple soulmates. I believe that each of us will find that one (or if you are incredibly lucky, then more than one) person who makes us want to continue living. For me, that person is you.

No, seriously, I'm not kidding. You, Veera, are definitely my soulmate.

And that is what makes it so hard for me to see you postpone dealing with your feelings, hoping that they'll eventually go away! You thought that no one noticed you today, that no one would see your smile was sad, that no one would ever know that you, too, crave comfort and a feeling of being wanted.

The whole day, while we ran around trying to make things work for Kavya and Siddharth, you were down. I know, it sucks to see everyone going all lovey-dovey when both of us are single. But none of us could brighten your mood.

And then when we were having ice cream outside school and you didn't have money to pay the shopkeeper, and Siddharth offered to pay for you, your mood went from zero to 100 in, like, three seconds.

Good things do happen, you know? You can't be living your life too afraid to get comfortable around people because you are so afraid they'll leave. Can you look me in the eye and tell me that if today Siddharth suddenly were to go out of your life forever, you wouldn't care at all? Actually, don't even answer that question. I already know the answer.

Whenever I've spoken about Siddharth to you, you've always brought up how hard it is to be friends with him and how much he infuriates you. It's almost like you don't allow yourself to think of him because you know that if you start you'll never stop. Why is it so hard for you to admit that he's important to you?

I'm not saying you like him. I'm saying that if someone is that important to you, then don't risk losing them just because they think you don't care enough! And it's almost scary how similar you guys are! You both suck at consoling others. If someone (other than me, of course) is crying, you guys will probably tell them to man the hell up and deal with it. Lol.

You are good for him. He is good for you. But you never open up to him fully because, face it, Veera, you are just too scared that he'll walk out of your life if you do that.

And don't give me that bullshit about how 'he is like that with everybody'.

You don't see it, but he treats you differently. First of all, he respects you, and for Siddharth Ahuja to respect someone, that person has to be pretty damn brilliant. And what do you do? You fight with him after he pays for your ice cream and lifts your mood. And why did you fight? Because he gave Niharika a rose (that he found on the freaking ground). Even Kavya wasn't pissed. And you didn't even tell him why you were annoyed!

If I know you, and I do know you, you are probably sulking this very instant about your argument. Has he called you yet? I hope he hasn't. For once, do yourself a favour and call him up first, will you? He always calls you.

Hahaha, it's funny how I'm giving real-time advice in a letter you'll probably never read.

To end this, I just want to tell you what a phenomenal person you are. It's a fucking honour to be your best friend. I know that you don't think of yourself as good enough—BUT. YOU. ARE. Though don't forget, hearts are often broken by words unspoken.

Love,
Ananya

She hadn't expected the words to be so soothing. Ananya was practically scolding her, but her words had had the desired effect. She remembered that day perfectly.

Veera had been so upset that Ananya had taken her out to a café after school.

As she'd sat, stirring her drink glumly, Ananya had sighed theatrically and sat up straighter, making Veera look up. They had just stared at each other for a few seconds, before Ananya dropped her gaze and a tiny smile tugged at her lips.

'What?' Veera had asked.

'I can't believe I'm going to say this,' Ananya had said, scraping her hair back from her face, 'but you'll go crazy without Siddharth in your life.'

Veera had burst out laughing. 'Yeah, sure.'

Veera Vishwanathan didn't *depend* on people. Depending on people led to weaknesses, and weaknesses could be exploited. It had happened with Mahir and it wouldn't happen again. No, Veera had only one weakness and that was Ananya. Because what was the point of happiness when it never lasted anyway?

What Ananya had said . . . could that be true? Could she really not imagine life without Siddharth?

She found herself automatically reaching for her phone and dialling Siddharth's number.

'The number that you are currently trying to reach is busy. Please hold the line or try again later.'

She ended the call instantly and flung her phone on the bed. What was she thinking? That Siddharth would actually be lying awake, waiting for her call? That he had nothing better to do than deal with her nonsense?

Her phone rang.

'Whom were you talking to?' That was the first thing he asked.

Veera frowned. She had expected an apology. 'Me? Whom were *you* talking to? Not that it matters to me . . .'

'I was trying to call *you*!'

'And I was trying to call *you*!'

Both of them burst out laughing, which sort of petered out into an uncomfortable silence.

Veera took a deep breath. 'I'm sorry,' she said in a squeaky voice.

'What? I didn't catch that,' Siddharth replied.

'I said, I'm sorry. I shouldn't have yelled at you,' Veera repeated.

'Nope, still can't hear you. Louder, please.' This time Veera detected a hint of laughter in his voice.

'You idiot,' she laughed, trying to be angry, 'you heard it perfectly the first time.'

'What was I supposed to do? Veera Vishwanathan doesn't usually apologize to me! It's a historic moment. And I just wanted to commit it to memory,' he laughed. 'The last time you apologized was—'

'Last Valentine's Day, I know,' Veera grimaced. 'Let's not make it a practice—what? I can't hear you.'

'I said, you were so jealous last year.'

'What! Of course not!' Veera was grateful that Siddharth couldn't see her face.

'Admit it,' Siddharth teased. 'You wanted to stab Niharika. I could see it in your eyes.'

'Bullshit,' Veera scoffed.

'But just saying, you don't have any reason to be jealous. I'm all yours.'

'Yuck! Thanks for the offer, but no thanks,' Veera laughed.

'Ouch, you break my heart, Subhu.'

'Call me that once more and your heart isn't the only thing I'll break.'

Siddharth laughed. There was a comfortable silence for a few minutes. Veera lay back on her bed, staring at her ceiling. Last summer, Veera and Ananya had decorated her ceiling. They had taken all the pictures of them they could find and pasted them randomly on the ceiling. The result was a crazy hotchpotch of photographs with hearts drawn in silver and gold, and silly quotes and lyrics written all over. She was so lost in thought that she almost missed it when Siddharth spoke again.

'Hey, Veera, is your dad an astronaut?'

'What?' Veera asked, confused.

''Cause you're a star,' he laughed.

'Oh my God, that was terrible!' Veera laughed nonetheless.

'The force of my attraction to you cannot be measured in Newton.'

'Stop!'

'Did you survive Avada Kedavra? Because you're drop-dead gorgeous.'

'Harry Potter pick-up line! Wow, someone upped their game.'

'Yeah right, my game was always up.'

'Okay, goodnight . . . or good morning. I'm going to sleep.' Veera sighed. She didn't want to stop talking to him but her eyes were shutting with exhaustion.

'You must be my Horcrux, because you complete me,' Siddharth laughed softly.

'Or, I'll be the cause of your death,' she said, smiling.

'Ain't that the truth,' Siddharth whispered, almost inaudibly, just before the line went dead. Veera smiled. How much better she felt now.

Study leave started tomorrow and after that were the finals. She had so much catching up to do. And then, after a week's break, they would be in the twelfth. There were a hundred things she had to do, a thousand things she had to say, but just for tonight, everything felt fine.

Nikhil

The Class-XI final exams were a weird time. Everyone wanted them to end and yet not end. The last exam meant freedom, parties and finally getting some sleep. But it also meant that there was nothing standing between them and the final year of school.

The rest of February sped past, drowned in the frustrated sighs of students, gigantic doses of caffeine and lack of sleep. But hey, what was high school without a mental breakdown every two or three days?

What starts eventually ends and so did the exams. And then almost immediately, without any time to brace oneself, it was judgement day—results. Nikhil trudged to school on Open House Day, thinking about the terminals and dreading what was to come.

He *hated* exams. Especially exam mornings, when he came to school worried out of his mind and completely unprepared. And filled with the anticipation that gnawed at his insides until he was ready to explode with the anxiety.

'I'll be fine, even if I haven't finished the portions, I've done all the chapters before and I believe in my powers of retention.' He had chanted this like a mantra over and over again. 'What's the worst that could happen?'

Well, for starters, you could not know a single thing in the paper and even mess up the few things you do know, the voice in his head had answered. *Also, maybe you won't finish the paper on time and then get such pathetic marks that you'll be ashamed to show your face in public. . . you'll always be a disappointment to your parents . . . and no one wants to associate themselves with a loser . . . so yeah . . . I'd say things CAN go wrong.* Anxiety is great at motivational speeches.

If Nikhil hated the mornings of the exams, Ananya loved them. Nikhil and Ananya were very different and that's exactly what Nikhil loved about her. She disagreed with most of his views but never imposed her views on him. She didn't dismiss him as a freak, and most of all, she took everything that bothered him seriously. Nikhil respected her . . . and it was hard for him, who hated all of humanity for its hypocrisy and false morals, to respect anyone.

'Don't you enjoy the mornings before an exam?' she had asked him one day, as they sat cross-legged on the floor, studying outside the examination hall. They'd reached early that day, and there were only a few people around.

This remark had annoyed Nikhil. There he was, furiously trying to cram some bull about the isomers of butane and pentane, already making up his mind that he was not going to pass that day, and here she was, being so annoyingly optimistic.

'You're prepared for the stupid exam. That's why you love this morning,' Nikhil had replied sourly, tugging at his hair.

'"That's why you love this morning",' she had mimicked. 'Will you stop doing that to your hair! You won't have any left . . . It's not like you have too much anyway . . .'

Nikhil had shot her a dirty look.

'Someone's cranky,' she'd mocked gently. 'What, did someone finally tell you that you can't rap in the exam hall?'

'IT CALMS ME, OKAY,' he'd half-yelled, but he'd been trying to hide a smile.

She'd continued, undeterred. 'Okay, first off, I'm not prepared . . . and for some reason, I can't be bothered to care. And second, being prepared has nothing to do with me liking this morning. I love the feeling of unity I get when I walk into the place and see everyone sharing knowing smiles, and realize I'm not the only one getting screwed. It's the students against the education system. Everyone loves everyone else during exams because we can all relate to the nervousness, the lack of sleep, the dark circles and the losing of our minds. And it's great to know that you're not the only one freaking out. No, don't look at me like that, Nikhil—I'm not a sadist.'

Nikhil hadn't been looking at her sceptically at all, but rather in amused wonder. He had shaken his head and said, 'What the fuck goes on in that brain of yours?'

'Shut the book. You'll be fine!' She'd grabbed his notes and stuffed them in his bag.

'You get good marks all the time! Let me study, fool!' Nikhil had yelled. 'How can you be so sure I'll be fine?'

'I just know,' she'd said, almost defiantly. 'You'll kill it.'

And he had felt slightly better after that.

Now, as he waited for his turn to meet the teacher at the Open House, he smiled. He didn't remember if he'd scored well or not in that exam, and he sure as hell didn't remember a thing about butane or pentane, but he remembered exactly what Ananya had said—word for word. Exam mornings didn't seem so bad when you looked at them like that.

Half an hour later he was out of school, holding his report card—he had stood fifth in class and he was elated. Siddharth had come first in Nikhil's class and Veera and Aakash had come first in their respective classes. Nikhil was happy for them.

He walked home quickly, eager to show his parents his report. Parents were usually required to accompany the student to Open House but Nikhil's parents never did. His father was a big shot in the scientific world. He spent a lot of his time peering down microscopes, and was respected as some sort of genius. Everyone except his father himself seemed to think that Nikhil had taken after him.

'Mom!' Nikhil yelled, letting himself into his house. 'See this!'

He almost ran into the living room, where his parents sat reading the paper. His father even *looked* like a scientist—thin and tall, with wire-rimmed glasses on his beady eyes—the kind they show in the movies. His mom was a banker, more corporate-looking—thin lips, rigid posture, and almost always impeccably dressed.

He held the report card out to his parents with a smile. 'Fifth,' he said triumphantly, as his father snatched the card from his hand. His mother smiled and pulled him in for a hug. But Nikhil watched his father's face carefully—it was his reaction that he wanted to see.

It never came. After a few minutes of strained silence, a minute sigh escaped from his father's lips. Finally, he stopped examining the report card and looked up.

'Hmmm, this is . . . nice,' he said, with a smile so fake that Nikhil wanted to gag.

'Nice?' Nikhil lowered his voice, trying to keep his anger in check. 'That's it? That's all you're going to say?'

'Oh, I'm sorry. Did you expect me to throw you a party for coming fifth?' He spat the word 'fifth' out like an insult.

Nikhil narrowed his eyes. 'What is wrong with standing fifth in class? I admit, it's not as great as the Top Three, but it really shows progress on my part!'

His father snorted dismissively.

'Wow, it's really hard for you to be happy for me, isn't it?' Nikhil blinked. How could he have not seen this coming? The fact that he genuinely expected his father to pat him on the back and say that he was proud of him made him feel like an idiot.

'Nikhil! Don't use that tone with your father,' his mother said sharply.

'Seriously?' Nikhil raised an eyebrow. 'What about the way he's talking to me?'

'Coming fifth isn't the same as standing first. Who came first?' his father asked, ignoring Nikhil's remark.

'Siddharth.'

'I knew it. He always works harder.'

Nikhil gritted his teeth. 'You are really making me hate Siddharth right now.'

'Nikhil, Rajesh, stop it,' his mom warned, her voice slightly higher than before.

'Look at him! Not even ashamed. With a rank like that it's better not to get one!' Rajesh waved the report card in his face like it was some scandalous article. Then under his breath he muttered, 'What a failure!'

Something inside Nikhil snapped. He looked down for a second to compose himself. His expression morphed into an emotionless mask. This was his fault. Why had he expected to have a civil conversation with his father anyway? He was an idiot for allowing himself to hope. But Nikhil learnt from his mistakes quickly.

He looked up and smiled widely because he knew it would infuriate his father.

'I will not be ashamed of doing my best and standing fifth in class. I will not hate my friends because you compare them with me.' He tilted his head slightly for effect, giving his father the strongest look of disdain he could muster. 'And as for being a failure, Dad, the apple doesn't fall far from the tree, does it? You are a failure as a father. I was bound to be one as a son.'

And with that he turned and walked away, leaving his parents scandalized and fuming. A crumpled report card hit the back of his head, but he kept walking. And when he reached his room, he didn't slam the door, he didn't yell and scream. He just quietly slipped inside and locked himself in.

As soon as the lock clicked behind him, he slumped to the floor, his head in his hands. He knew that in about half an hour his mother would come knocking on the door, demanding that he come out and make up with his father.

He sighed. This had happened so many times that Nikhil was almost immune to it—but not quite. Rajesh Shetty was a genius and his son was not. And that would forever grate on his father's nerves.

Relationships had never worked out for Nikhil. And when he couldn't handle relationships in his own home, how could he ever hope to find love outside? From a very young age he had learnt that he could never please his father. The constant pressure and fights turned him into the brooding 'weirdo' whom no one could understand or even wanted to.

Finally he'd decided that if people wanted to talk about him, he would give them something to talk about. His upbringing had resulted in him seeing the world in black and white. Either you were worth his time, or you weren't. Either he agreed with your views or he didn't. Nikhil never understood why his father was on his case every single second of every single day, and in the bid to find an answer to this he'd begun questioning everything in his life. Without an explanation that satisfied him, he wouldn't accept anything. Questioning became second nature to him. Moral values were stupid. When there's no praise for doing the right things, and only punishment for all the wrongs, why be good at all?

Searching for stability in his life, he'd embraced the one thing in life that promised to remain constant—Science. Science was rational. Science didn't suddenly start acting weird without a proper explanation. Science had taught him that there was a reason for everything, and to not have unrealistic expectations. And Science had soon led him into the arms of atheism, much to the distress of his mother, who was a staunch believer in God.

Science was also the one connection that he had with his father.

He pulled himself up from the floor and turned off the lights. And as the darkness closed in around him, his room glowed with a million words. Despite his grim mood, he smiled.

Scrawled across his walls, ceiling and even the floor, in large letters, in neon pink, yellow, orange and green, was every English swear word one could think of.

On his twelfth birthday, Nikhil had decided to redecorate his room. His parents had both been out of town and his grandparents were looking after him.

He had painted his entire room black, and with white he had painted every English swear word he knew. He'd even looked some up.

What twelve-year-old decorated his bedroom with curse words, right? Many may call it self-expression, rebellion or some other such bullshit, but for Nikhil Shetty it was purely a scientific endeavour.

Needless to say, his parents were horrified when they came back and saw what they considered vandalism and blatant disrespect. His father had dragged him into the room by his collar and yelled for an explanation.

'Experiments show that swearing relieves pain and helps you calm down, it's a great stress buster and also increases your threshold for pain. Since I'm not allowed to swear, I did the next best thing,' Nikhil had explained, unruffled. The next second, his face was stinging from his father's slap.

That was the first time his father had slapped him, and Nikhil had been shocked. He'd spent the next two days scrubbing his room clean and chanting mantras for purification that his grandparents had insisted on. For the first time, Nikhil had been truly disgusted with his father. And from then on, he'd stopped trying to gain his father's approval. Every little thing he said or did was an act of rebellion and defiance.

He'd repainted his walls with invisible paint that only showed up in the dark and left it like that—an open invitation, a challenge. Of course, his father knew about this. And every time he'd got rid of the obscenities, Nikhil had redone his walls just as quickly. Soon enough, it had morphed into an ego battle between the two of them. It was exhausting to paint his room over and over, but Nikhil was not about to back down.

Sitting in the dim glow of these words gave Nikhil some relief.

Okay, no point sitting here sulking.

He grabbed his phone to see if his friends wanted to hang out.

'Aakash . . . Anany—'

He was scrolling through his contact list, and seeing her name, he swallowed his feelings and continued. 'Aslesha . . . Siddharth . . . Veera . . . No, none of them.' He checked their WhatsApp group and saw that all of them were busy shopping or preparing for the day trip that they were supposed to take later that week, to Siddharth's farmhouse.

It was a short weekend trip. They planned to stay the night and return the next day. Siddharth's aunt and uncle lived in the villa next to the farmhouse, and so, after much pleading and careful manipulation, all their parents had agreed. Aslesha had begged and pleaded till Siddharth had agreed to call Kavya too. For the first time, Mahir was coming along with them as well. Somehow, over the course of these few months, Mahir had melded into their group and no one knew how that had happened. Maybe it was because of the weird deal between him and Aakash, but it didn't really matter. It was kind of nice to have him around.

He set his phone down and leaned back against the wall. A minute later he thought about meeting the one person he knew would have finished packing as well as double- and triple-checking her to-pack checklist.

It just showed how desperate he was for company, and how willing to talk about shoes.

Before he had even finished making up his mind, he was slamming the main door shut behind him, vaguely wondering if anyone had ever actually died of boredom.

Kavya

Kavya was having a perfectly peaceful day. Until the doorbell rang.

'No,' she said, when she opened the door and spotted him.

'But I haven't even said anything yet!' Nikhil whined.

'Okay, let's see.' Kavya leaned on her door. 'Have you come to confess your undying love for me?'

Nikhil's forehead creased. 'Um . . . no.'

'Have you brought chocolate?'

'What?' He was looking at her weirdly. 'Are you serious? I mean, what?'

'Yeah, thought so,' Kavya sighed. 'Well, if it's none of these, then the answer to whatever it is you want is no.'

'Oh, shut up.' Nikhil rolled his eyes. 'Besides, why would you want me to confess my "undying love" for you?'

'Heh,' she shrugged. 'Okay, bye.' She was about to shut the door, but was unnerved by Nikhil's stare.

'Oh my God!' Kavya exclaimed in mock outrage. 'Stop checking me out.'

Nikhil didn't even flinch. With a lazy raise of his eyebrows, he said, 'Give your tiny brain a rest, will you. I was just trying to remember why I thought it made sense to come here.' After a brief pause he added, 'Although, now that you've brought it up . . .' He made a show of looking her up and down. 'Nice shorts!'

Kavya rolled her eyes but couldn't help smiling slightly. 'Yeah, go for it. And if your brain can multitask, do tell me why you're here.'

'I thought you didn't want to know?'

'I changed my mind.'

'Let's go for a walk.'

'What, no! I don't do walks.' She crinkled her nose in disdain.

'Yeah, well, you "do walks" now. Come on.' He turned and started walking without waiting for her, and she wondered why he was so sure she would follow. After hesitating a moment, she shut the door behind her and caught up with him near the elevator.

'Wow, that was fast,' he said teasingly, as she tied her hair into a high ponytail and jogged after him.

She pressed the lift button. 'So . . . what do you think?' she asked, striking a pose.

His eyes skimmed over her briefly.

'I've seen better,' he said, as the lift door opened and he walked in, the ghost of a smile flitting across his face.

By the time Kavya could pick up her jaw from the ground, the lift had dinged shut. Nikhil, being the gentleman that he was, obviously hadn't held the door for her, and she was forced to wait for the second lift to arrive. Although she was sorely tempted to just abandon him and go back home, where she could relax and stuff her face with ice cream while binge watching *Gossip Girl*, she decided she couldn't let him show her up her like that.

When the lift door opened, Nikhil stood outside, looking annoyed, like *he* had the right to be annoyed.

'So where are we going?' Kavya asked, falling into step beside him as they exited her building.

'I don't know,' he grumbled.

'Okay, if you're going to be grumpy the whole way then bye, I'm going back.' She turned to walk back the way they had come when Nikhil caught her wrist and pulled her back.

'Sorry,' he sighed. 'It's just . . . it's been a bad day.'

For the first time, a look of genuine understanding softened her features. 'Ah, results. Hard luck this time?'

Nikhil glanced up, amused. He hadn't expected her to understand what he'd been trying to say. 'No, not really. Came fifth.'

'Wow!' Kavya placed her hand on her heart in mock sympathy. 'It *really* must suck to get a rank.'

'Shut up,' he grumbled. 'It's not me, it's my dad.'

'I haven't heard that excuse before,' Kavya laughed. 'What happened?'

'Does it really matter to you?' Nikhil asked.

'Are you kidding?' Kavya said. 'I'm in it for the drama.'

'My dad's always on my case, you know? Nothing's ever good enough for him.' They had reached Carter Road by now and were walking aimlessly. 'As far as he's concerned, coming fifth is a cardinal sin.'

Kavya was quiet.

Nikhil continued. 'And the worst part is how he's always comparing me to my friends!'

'No, I get it,' Kavya said, looking at him. 'It sucks to have overachieving friends. Here—let's sit down. I'm wearing flats and I don't like being so close to the ground while standing.'

She dragged him to a bench that overlooked the sea as Nikhil burst out laughing.

'That is the stupidest thing I've ever heard!'

They sat down, his arm resting on the bench top, as she leaned back and turned to face him.

'Sometimes—' Kavya started, and Nikhil rolled his eyes. 'What!'

'You started with "sometimes" . . . People usually start that way when they're planning to say some stupid pretentious shit.'

'Okay, rule number one: don't interrupt; and rule number two: don't be an asshole,' Kavya chuckled. 'So as I was saying, sometimes parents try to keep stress levels super high so that even if we disregard most of what they say, we'll retain some of the stress, which will hopefully motivate us into working harder than we're likely to on our own. They believe in the whole coal-under-too-much-pressure-turns-into-diamond bullshit. They just overdo it sometimes. But then again, parents are known for their messed-up logic.'

'That does make sense, actually . . .' Nikhil smiled. 'But I feel like I can't really forgive him. I can't let it go.'

'No one said you have to let it go, like, right now.' She flipped her hair and turned to face the sea. 'Chances are, they don't even know how you feel.'

'How can they not know how I feel?' Nikhil suddenly looked agitated. He sat up straight, throwing his hands up. 'Can't they see it?'

Kavya reached out and clasped his wrists, mostly because their frantic movements were annoying her. A minute of heavy silence passed.

'Now that you're calm again,' Kavya said cautiously, letting go of his wrists and exhaling, 'you have to see how it probably looks to them. To them, you are a teenager hell-bent on doing everything he's told not to do.'

'Lack of communication, huh?' Nikhil scoffed. 'That's been a problem since I was born. But I still blame him. He's slapped me, man.'

Oh my God, this boy is so stubborn. She blew a strand of hair out of her face.

'Okay,' she said, setting her jaw. 'You're right. Your dad is horrible.'

'What?' Nikhil stared at her in confusion.

'No, really. Your family is messed-up, dude. Your childhood must've been traumatic!' She winced for effect.

'It wasn't that bad . . .' Nikhil blinked, trying to understand the sudden shift.

'Of course it was! You must hate your dad!' she said. Oh God, she definitely had a death wish. 'Let him go to hell.'

'Hey! Enough!' Nikhil's eyes were suddenly dark with anger.

'But you said that he always gave you a hard time! What a despicable man!' She had to push him just a little more.

And then suddenly Nikhil was so close to Kavya that she forgot how to breathe.

'That man . . . is my father.' Nikhil's voice was a whisper. 'He may not be perfect—whoever he is and however he is—but at the end of the day he's my father, and he's taught me more than I can begin to imagine. So, I appreciate your effort but I will not have him insulted by someone who is not even half as smart as he is.'

Despite her best efforts, she felt a little hurt. But she swallowed hard, trying not to think about the lack of distance between them, and smiled. Smiled so widely that it threw Nikhil off.

'There you go,' she said, a hint of triumph in her tone.

'What?' he almost spat at her.

'You *defended* him. That guy that you "hate" so much? You just instinctively defended him,' she said.

'What are y—oh.' Realization flooded through him. 'No—but that was . . . ugh. Obviously I would defend him against a third party! It doesn't prove anything!'

'Of course it does! You love him. You admire him. And you crave his approval. But he doesn't know that. The people you love don't necessarily have to say good things to your face, but they'll say the good stuff when you aren't there to hear it. Your dad wasn't here; there was no need to defend him . . . but you did.' She sighed. 'Sorry I insulted him so much—but you're so dense, I had to!'

The expression on his face was worth it. He tilted his head slightly and fixed her with that unnerving stare of his. Then his face broke into the most wonderful smile ever.

'Wow, *now* I get a genuine smile,' she grumbled, and Nikhil chuckled.

'Have you ever considered a career in psychology?' he asked, still smiling.

'Many times,' she laughed. 'I would be a boon to all the socially challenged people out there.'

He lowered his eyes. 'What I said earlier about you not being smart enough . . .'

'Mmmh? You have really long eyelashes . . . Oh, wait, you said something?' Kavya looked up, expecting Nikhil to laugh, but he was still looking down. 'Oh God, it's fine. I didn't take it personally! Plus, I'll have you know that I came third in class.'

Nikhil's eyes shot up. 'Really?'

'Really.'

'But I'm sorry, still. It must be annoying to get stereotyped all the time—pretty and popular, and so *obviously*, not smart, right? I'm just sorry I added to that, though I swear I don't think of you that way. Also, contrary to popular belief, I'm not always judging people!'

Oh. Wow.

Kavya stared at him. All her life she'd had to work extra hard to be taken seriously. People assumed that she didn't have any right to complain, that she had no problems in her life, because she was good-looking. If she cribbed about something, they passed snide remarks like 'Wow, it must be so hard to be gorgeous'. Boys were no different. They either assumed she was a pushover or, if she didn't show interest, they thought she was playing hard to get. Her opinions weren't valued because everyone just *assumed* she wasn't smart. She spoke about shoes, clothes and parties. Well, that just meant that she knew how to take pleasure in the small joys of life. It didn't mean she was stupid or that her views were irrelevant.

Nikhil had summed it up effortlessly, and with so much sincerity.

She saw that Nikhil was freaking out a bit and realized that she was staring.

She smiled and dramatically said, 'Society doesn't like those who are sure of themselves.' Then after a pause she added, 'You don't do this often, do you?'

'Apologizing? Nah, it's not my thing,' he grinned. 'But I meant it.'

'Pretty impressive, apology accepted! Though I have no clue how you came up with all that without me even saying a word,' she said. 'You seem to be giving me competition in psychoanalysis.'

'Nope, I think you got it covered.'

Someone cleared their throat in front of them and Kavya froze.

She immediately became aware of how close she and Nikhil were, their faces inches apart and legs almost touching. Nikhil hadn't pulled away after the whole reverse-psychology episode. His eyes never left her face and she couldn't look away. But she had to. What if it was someone they knew?

Annoyance flashed across Nikhil's face as he registered the presence of the intruder. He slowly pulled away, trying to look nonchalant.

Nothing had been interrupted.

Just pointless banter.

Right.

Kavya turned to see who it was—and wanted to disappear.

'Siddharth,' Nikhil said, swallowing and trying to smile. He still looked a little confused. He always looked confused. Kavya smiled at the thought in spite of herself.

Siddharth looked visibly uncomfortable. 'I was just passing by and I saw you guys, so just thought I'd come over and say hi . . . Think I'll just go—bye!'

'No, wait!' Nikhil, that idiot, called after him. 'Congrats for coming first, man!'

'What? Oh, that.' He smiled. 'Thanks! Same to you . . . both. I heard you came third, Kavya.'

'Yes, I did, thank you . . . Right, Siddharth, you wanted to ask me about that thing, right?'

'What thing?'

'*That* thing! You said you had to talk urgently about it, remember?'

'I . . . I did? Oh, oh right! I did!'

'I'll be back in a minute,' she told Nikhil, as she grabbed Siddharth's arm and dragged him to the side.

'What?'

'What?' Siddharth struggled to hide a smile.

'Don't "what" me! Why are you making that face, that expression, that *everything*?' Kavya frowned.

'Life is cruel.' Siddharth clicked his tongue. 'Also ironic.'

'I don't know what you're talking about.' Kavya massaged her temples.

'You fought with Veera because you saw me *comforting* her, and you flipped. Then you took the moral high ground and pretended we were all beneath you. And *now*,' he smiled wickedly, 'and now I see you gallivanting with Nikhil.' He wiggled his eyebrows suggestively.

Kavya rolled her eyes.

'Oh please, don't exert your tiny little brain so much. Nothing's happening. We just decided to go for a walk.'

'First, he was practically all over you! Second, oh, so he asked you out?' Siddharth grinned.

'No, God no! He was just dealing with some stuff and wanted someone to talk to.' She scowled.

'And he wanted to talk to you about it?' Siddharth raised his eyebrows.

Struck by the validity of the question, Kavya let the snide tone in Siddharth's voice slide.

'Yes, I'm a great psychiatrist, if I say so myself. Now bye, you have to go. And not another word about Nikhil and me, okay?'

She watched with mounting irritation as Siddharth raised his hands in mock surrender and walked away.

She leaned back against the wall and looked out at the sea. She was still annoyed at him and Veera. Maybe it was payback time . . . nothing serious, just something fun to keep her occupied. No guy would be comfortable with his ex-girlfriend getting too close to another guy so soon. Even if he wasn't jealous, it would irritate him, and that was enough for Kavya.

Obviously, Nikhil couldn't know.

But Siddharth was gone, and, at least for now, she could be herself. Before she put the horrible plan taking shape in her head into action.

As she was walking back, she saw Nikhil talking to a tall girl with flowing hair. Kavya recognized her instantly.

'What is this bitch doing here—OH MY GOD, HI! What a coincidence!' Kavya's voice changed as Niharika turned and saw her.

'I know, right!' Niharika gushed, and Kavya almost laughed out loud at the hatred she saw in Niharika's eyes. 'I can't believe we haven't spoken before! Anyway, nice running into you guys, I've got to rush! Bye!'

Keep your paws off him, bitch, Kavya thought savagely as she waved enthusiastically, a brilliant smile plastered on her face.

Once Niharika was gone and the two of them began walking home, Nikhil asked, 'Why did you do that?'

'Do what?'

'Why were you nice?' he asked as if that was a totally legit question.

Kavya laughed. 'Why is that a bad thing?'

'No, I mean why were you nice to her when you clearly wanted to strangle her?' Nikhil continued to sound serious.

'That's just the way it is,' Kavya said airily.

Nikhil caught her wrist, stalling her. 'Be a bitch by all means, but don't be fake.' He let her hand go and walked ahead.

It took Kavya a minute to register what he'd said but she pushed it away. Jogging to catch up with him, she huffed, 'Can I ask you something?'

'You already have.' His lips twitched.

She rolled her eyes. 'Lame. Why did you call me? Of all the people you could've spoken to, when you were annoyed?'

'Because I knew you would've finished packing and would be free.' She knew he was only teasing her, but she dropped the subject. Maybe because she couldn't think of an answer to her own question. She didn't like being with *herself* when she was pissed off, so why would anyone else?

The next time Nikhil spoke, they were in the lift of Kavya's building.

'I don't know, actually,' he said, picking up the conversation exactly where it had been left off. Kavya realized that he had been giving the question serious thought this entire time. 'It's just . . . you make my problems seem insignificant.'

Kavya's eyebrows rose up. That wasn't the answer she'd been expecting at all. 'And that is a good thing because . . .?'

Nikhil laughed. 'I guess it sounded stupid when I said it like that. I meant that they don't seem so big after talking to you. They seem more like something I can deal with, as opposed to something I've blown ridiculously out of proportion. You're just so caught up in the moment that sometimes I want to live like that with you, in the present, instead of constantly scrambling towards an uncertain future. Also, you aren't dismissive and, for some reason, actually seem to be fine with me being my usual horrible self.'

'With,' Kavya muttered softly as the lift dinged open. 'You said you want to live *with* me in the present.'

'Of course, I meant "like",' he said a bit too hurriedly. 'I meant I want to live *like* you in the present.'

Kavya leaned against her door when they reached her house and extended her hand. 'Nikhil Shetty, know that you had the pleasure of spending an entire evening in the company of this wonderful lady. You are most welcome.'

Swiftly, before Kavya even realized it, Nikhil took her hand and, instead of shaking it, brushed his lips against it in the lightest of kisses. As he dropped her hand, she gasped.

'The pleasure is all mine,' he said.

'A bit too excited, are we?' Kavya kept her tone light, trying to recover her composure.

Nikhil grinned and shrugged. 'Just playing the part!' He turned to go and she stood leaning against her door frame, her brown eyes following him. Just before the lift door opened, he called out, 'You know, I don't think I've met one of you before.'

'One of what?' Kavya asked, just as he entered the lift.

'A walking contradiction.'

And she could almost hear the smile in his voice as the lift shut.

Nikhil

Nikhil,

'Sometimes the only pay-off for having any faith is when it's tested again and again, every day.'

Remember that? That song is old now, but the lyrics are so potent. I know what you see when you look at yourself in the mirror. But when I look at you, you know what I see? (Please pardon me for sounding like a mother, lol, I'm sorry XD) I see an extremely smart, strong guy who will always stand by his beliefs, no matter what. A guy who will always be there for his friends. There aren't enough of you in this world and so the world doesn't know how to handle you.

I remember telling you that I want to write about you, and the first thing you asked me was, 'What could you possibly write about me?'

So here I am, writing to you, and about you, on results day. I saw how your face fell when you came ninth last year. I know you're worried about the future. I know you think that you are a failure. And it makes me laugh. Why? Because out of all of us here, you should be the one least concerned. I look at you, and when I see how dejected you are, I can't but feel a little helpless. How can you not see how successful you are going to be in life? How can you not see how smart you are? How can you not see that even though you think of yourself as some kind of rebel, you follow every rule, keep every promise and end up doing the right thing even if it's the hard thing?

I love how your eyes light up even when you talk about the most inane things you're passionate about. I don't even like rap music, but when you talk about what it means to you, I feel like there's more to it. You think kindness is against evolution and yet I haven't actually ever seen you be unkind (I don't mean rude— you are almost always rude) to anyone. You criticize but also compliment freely. You have no idea how much it means to me to have you as a friend.

I know you think that you don't deserve my friendship. You think I'm some sort of mahatma who is always 'helping' you. But I don't know if you even know the number of things you've done for me without even realizing it. You helped me see things from different perspectives, you didn't dismiss my issues, you didn't think I was a mess. When I got bad marks, you pushed me to do better. You knew how much it freaked me out to speak in front of an audience, and every time I had to make a presentation or took part in a debate, you were there five minutes early to give me a pep talk. In a weird way, we look out for each other, and that's something I genuinely enjoy.

Nikhil Shetty is well on his way to being successful in whatever the fuck he chooses to do. I know this with such finality that I'm 100 per cent convinced that in the time to come, I'll be telling people I used to be in school with THE Nikhil Shetty. Just please do me a favour and believe in yourself and stop pushing people away? You do not ruin whatever you touch. That's just stupid.

And as for your parents? Nobody is going to be able to boost your self-esteem, except you. In this world that's constantly trying to make you someone else, being yourself is the biggest accomplishment (I stole that from Ralph Waldo Emerson—I seriously love that guy).

I don't guarantee that you will never get hurt. The only choice you'll have in the matter is to decide if it's worth it. When someone is rude to you or challenges your beliefs, you get super defensive. And even after the matter has been sorted out, you take a looong time to let things go. Why? Why hold grudges and ruin your existence? Plus, forgiveness gets on people's nerves like nothing else! Bad decisions make for good stories. You're going to have a grrreat life—I KNOW it. And it's high time you started believing it too.

I've ended up writing so much when what I wanted to say was this: Blast your rap music, kill all your tests, use your defiance as a motivator and fuck everyone who says 'you can't'. Keep being you and keep being my friend (lol). We all know that you are already sorted into the successful pile.

Love,
Ananya.

P.S: I love your room. I wish I could do that too! Hahaha. Just kidding, I'm a sanskari child, you know me!

When Nikhil put the letter down, he was smiling. He wasn't crying, he wasn't depressed . . . he was actually happy. Trust Ananya to do this. Who the fuck wrote a letter like this—so stupidly silly and yet so serious? It felt like she was right there, talking to him. This had been written a year ago, in slightly different circumstances, but her words still rang true. They were unbelievably refreshing, and for the first time in ages, the bone-deep tiredness he'd been feeling faded slightly.

He stood up and stretched. *Sanskari, my ass.* He couldn't help grinning at that.

She believed in him. Her conviction was like a cool, calming breeze. She had spoken about his success like it was the most obvious thing, like there could be no two ways about it. And he loved her for it. She'd believed in him this much when he thought he'd given her no reason to—he couldn't be all that useless then, could he?

The void of Ananya's death had faded slightly. He hadn't expected to feel this happy after reading the letter. But it had really made him feel like she was still around . . . that she was still with him.

He remembered talking to Ananya last year at the Open House about what the future had in store for them. Ananya wanted to study in the US, while Nikhil, in his characteristic bid to be different, had declared that he wanted to study in Singapore. Ananya had laughed, saying that it would be cool to have friends in different continents.

'And just imagine, when you're all rich and have a mansion and stuff, and are settled in Singapore, I can come visit,' she had said.

'Visit? Like a guest? Like once in two years or something? Fuck off!' He'd rolled his eyes. 'I'll just call you randomly and be like, "Wanna have lunch today?" and then you'll fly down in your private jet from America to have lunch with me, and then we'll go sightseeing and then you can go back at night.'

'Deal! And then when you come to the US, I'll give you a shopping list of everything I want from Singapore.'

Nikhil had shuddered mockingly. 'Shopping for a *woman*? World-renowned millionaire will be checking things off a shopping list for a woman? You demean me.'

'Don't be sexist! World-renowned millionaire can do this much for his friends, okay?' She'd poked him indignantly.

He shook his head now, at the memories from that distant afternoon.

His thoughts flitted to Kavya.

He'd come back home and gone straight to his room. The lights in his room had come on, bright against the dark sky, the rebellion faded from his walls for a while. He'd had a surprisingly good time with Kavya. And as a bonus, she had mentioned shoes only *once*!

He glanced at his watch. 8.30 p.m. His mom and dad would already be having dinner downstairs. He had stopped eating with them ever since his dad had slapped him that first time. He sighed. Maybe it was Kavya's influence, or Ananya's letter, or perhaps both—but suddenly it all felt so far away.

Kavya's words came back to him. The coal-and-diamond logic. Could it be true? When was the last time he'd had a civil conversation with his dad? When was the last time they'd felt like a family? When was the last time he'd given them a chance?

Why hold grudges and poison your existence?

It was true. His whole existence had been poisoned by the grudge he'd held since as far back as he could remember. He knew what Ananya would want him to do if she were there. She would want him to go down and talk it out. Her solution was always to talk it out. If you asked her, she would probably say that the world's hunger problems could be ended by talking it out.

With a sigh he folded up the letter and stood up, unsure of exactly what he was setting himself up for.

His mother paused with her fork halfway to her mouth as she saw Nikhil walk up with his plate of food. Melodramatic? Maybe. Justified? Definitely.

The expression of incredulity that flitted across his dad's face when he sat down at the dining table made Nikhil grin. But he hid it quickly.

'Hi,' he said.

His parents stared.

'Okaaayy . . .' he went on, 'not what I was expecting, but I'll take it.'

Silence.

'Fine, I'll get to the point. God, you guys really are antisocial.' He thought he saw a ghost of a smile on his dad's face.

'I understand that, as parents, it must be hard to always be on my case, because, I guess, well, you're responsible for me. I'm sorry I acted out and rebelled against every small thing you guys wanted. It's just—I guess I wanted a little appreciation and a pat on the back once in a while. But honestly, I'm happy with the place I am at right now. And just because I'm content with right now does not mean that I'm overconfident. It does not mean that I'll stop pushing myself, okay? So don't mistake my laid-back appearance as not being serious. I'm sorry I'm not the son you hoped for—' His voice faltered. 'Dad, I know you think I'm not smart enough—'

'Smart enough?' Rajesh spoke for the first time. 'Is that what you think? That I think you're not smart enough? I know you're smart enough. Probably even smarter than me—maybe. And that is exactly why I'm always on your case. You know how it is these days—survival of the fittest. And I couldn't stand the thought that someone with your potential could become complacent.'

'What? But you *slapped* me, Dad!' Nikhil stared.

His dad rolled his eyes. 'I've only slapped you three times in my life. I'm sure you made it seem ten times worse in your head.'

Nikhil's forehead creased. Really? It seemed like he'd been pushed around way more. He saw his mother elbow his dad in the ribs.

'But . . . um . . .' he stammered, 'I'm sorry too. I know you lost your friend—she was a wonderful girl—and I shouldn't be so hard on you. The more you pulled away, the more I tried and couldn't connect with you—you have to understand that.'

'I do,' Nikhil nodded, stunned by his father's apology.

'I'm proud of you,' his dad said, and Nikhil looked up sharply.

'Okay, too much. You don't need to say that.'

'No, I'm serious. I've always been. Just because I haven't expressed it doesn't mean it's not true. The only thing that genuinely gets my goat is that room of yours.'

Nikhil burst out laughing, feeling lighter than he remembered feeling in years. His dad's lips twitched.

'We should take a picture—this is so touching,' his mom mocked sportingly. She went into the kitchen and returned with more food.

'So tell me,' his father said, swallowing a mouthful of dal chawal, 'now that we're having this father-son moment—do you have any girlfriends?'

Nikhil almost choked.

'Girlfriends?' his mom said, laughing. 'Are you suggesting that he has more than one?'

'Why not?' his dad continued, while Nikhil felt the little dignity he had squirming and fading away. 'He has that whole tortured-artist vibe going for him . . .'

He turned and saw Nikhil looking scandalized. 'What? Too soon?'

'Definitely!' he almost yelled. 'But no, I don't have a girlfriend.'

'That's why he's like this.' His mom hit her head, laughing. 'He needs a girl in his life.'

Nikhil groaned and stuffed his mouth with food to avoid replying. Really, what *had* he got himself into?

Mahir

'You guys brought something Indian to wear, right?' Mahir asked, helping Kavya load her giant suitcase into the back of the van. Road-trip day was here and Mahir couldn't be more excited.

'For the hundredth time, yes, Mahir, we did,' Siddharth replied, playing with his phone. Mahir figured that he was probably tweaking their playlist.

'I don't know why, though,' Veera said. 'Why would we need traditional clothes?'

'I know, I even packed beachwear . . . there is a beach nearby, right?' Kavya asked Mahir.

'No there isn't,' Nikhil replied. 'It's a farmhouse, not a resort.'

'But,' Mahir's eyes gleamed with humour, 'feel free to wear your *beachwear* around the house.'

Kavya smacked his arm but she was laughing. 'Jerk! Where's Aslesha? We're already running late.'

'I can't believe you guys made me get up at 5.30 in the morning. I could've slept an extra hour, at least,' Aakash grumbled, loading his bag into the van. 'This van is good, by the way.'

Mahir smiled in acknowledgement. He had organized the van so that they wouldn't have to split up in different cars. Half the fun of this trip lay in the journey.

'Hey, I can't help it if Kavya took so long to get ready!' Siddharth said, raising his hands in defence as Kavya shot him a dirty look. 'Oh look, Aslesha's here.'

Mahir laughed at Siddharth and Kavya as Aslesha loaded her bag into the van. To Mahir, it definitely looked like they were over each other, but it was also clear that Kavya hadn't forgiven him for initiating the break-up. Well, he didn't know what the reason was, but he sure was glad that they were being civil to each other at least for the road trip—Kavya was being civil even to Veera!

'Okay, one last thing before we go,' Aslesha said, narrowing her eyes. 'Today, people, is my no-lie day. I cannot and will not lie *at all* . . . it's a sort of personal pledge. Do not ask me how, what and why. So be nice and don't make this hard—'

'Who was your first crush?' Mahir asked.

'Whom do you like now?' asked Veera.

'Did you *actually* cheat in that maths test last year?' Aakash jumped in.

'What's the riskiest thing you've ever done?' Kavya piped up.

'I am, however, not obliged to answer any questions you put forth,' Aslesha answered cheerfully, as they all let out sighs of disappointment. 'But thanks, guys, it's nice to see all the support.'

Siddharth laughed. 'Okay, come on, let's go. Everyone in the van!'

Mahir watched, surprised, as Kavya grabbed Nikhil's hand. 'Come on! Let's get the best seats!'

Was he the only one who thought that was weird? He looked around and saw everyone looking at them funnily, including Siddharth, who looked confused. Poor Nikhil looked like a deer caught in the headlights.

Mahir caught Siddharth's eye and raised an eyebrow. Siddharth responded with an imperceptible shake of the head. *I don't know.*

Aslesha tensed visibly beside him. 'I cannot believe this,' she whispered through gritted teeth. 'She's trying to make him jealous!'

Oh. That made sense.

'Oh, um . . . sure . . .?' Nikhil's response sounded like a question. He looked at Kavya questioningly.

Aslesha coughed. 'Oh, sure. Leave the best friend for the guy. Classic Kavya!'

Kavya had the grace to blush. 'Aslesha!'

'No, no, don't mind me. I'll just sit alone . . . the *entire* way,' she said, lowering her head. Kavya groaned.

When Aslesha raised her head, she was smiling. 'I'm kidding! I call shotgun and I'm handling the music! Everyone get ready for a *real* education in music.' And she raced into the van.

'Guess that's our cue,' said Mahir, and the rest of them piled into the van.

Finally, Aakash got into the van, followed by Veera.

'Oh no, you don't,' Mahir said, just as Aakash started swinging himself into the seat next to Siddharth. 'You and I have a lot to talk about on this journey, my friend.' He grinned and patted the spot next to him. Aakash sighed and went to sit next to him. Veera sat down next to Siddharth, looking at Aakash quizzically.

When they were off at last, and Aslesha had settled into DJ mode, Veera finally spoke.

'Aakash,' she said, 'what is it that you're not telling us?'

'Nothing,' Aakash said with a straight face.

'Don't lie.' Siddharth turned to face him.

'No, I mean, I'm literally telling you guys nothing,' he laughed.

'Okay, let's enlighten them,' Mahir grinned. 'Ladies and gentlemen, our in-house entertainer today will be none other than—Aakash Acharya, who is going to be telling us about his life.'

There was a buzz of confusion. Mahir sighed. 'I'm friends with idiots. He's going to tell us about him and Ananya.'

At the mention of her name, Siddharth quickly glanced at Veera, and Kavya at Nikhil. They seemed to be fine. In fact, they'd all turned around in their seats to look at Aakash.

'Really?' Veera almost squealed, and Siddharth looked at her weirdly.

'What are you so excited about? You knew everything from the beginning anyway!' Siddharth said indignantly. 'I'm offended that Aakash is telling Mahir stuff after spending, like, two days with him, when he hasn't told *me*, his best friend, anything till now.'

'That's what happens when you're friends with *everyone*, Siddharth. You miss out sometimes,' Veera said slyly, and the whole van roared with laughter.

'Aloe vera, Siddharth? Because you just got hella burnt,' Aslesha yelled from the front and turned the volume on Gwen Stefani's 'Baby Don't Lie' higher, just to annoy him.

'She's a keeper!' Mahir yelled over the music and shut up immediately, as Veera and Kavya both narrowed their eyes at him.

'Okay, okay,' Siddharth conceded. 'I'll get back at you for that.'

'Would love to see you try,' she replied sweetly.

'Guys, guys. Stop stealing the limelight. Focus! This is Aakash's moment,' Nikhil grinned. 'So? What you waiting for? Begin!'

'It's not that simple,' Aakash said timidly. Then he glared at Mahir. 'I didn't know we were going to make this a public thing!'

'Pfft,' Mahir snorted. 'Don't be so dramatic.'

'Okay, fine. What do you guys want to know?' he asked resignedly.

'Everything!' Kavya shouted.

'Name *one* incident.' Aakash figured it would be harder for them to choose a specific incident. 'Oh God, Aslesha, can you stick to *one* song? You keep changing it every five seconds.'

'Don't rain on my parade, asshole,' Aslesha yelled, and then promptly changed the song.

'So?' Mahir looked around. They were sitting on the last seat and the rest of them had all turned around to face them. 'Any suggestions?'

'Oh, I know!' Veera suddenly said, bouncing up and down. She swatted Siddharth's hand away when he attempted to still her. Mahir couldn't help thinking how much better Veera looked since he had last seen her. She was finally healing, or at least trying to. 'Tell us about the first time you met her parents.'

'You met her parents?' Nikhil asked, outraged. 'You didn't tell me. Like, you officially met them? She introduced y'all and stuff? Was this before or after you guys were dating?'

'First, we were never dating. And second,' Aakash shot Veera a murderous look, 'I really, *really* hate you.'

'What's the big deal anyway? We've all met her parents,' Kavya said flippantly. 'It's different if you're dating. But even then, *some people* refuse to meet the parents,' she said pointedly.

'Hey!' Siddharth was indignant. 'I met your parents! Your mother hated me! I was obviously never "good enough for her perfect little daughter".' He did a ridiculous impression of her mom.

'Clearly, she was right,' Kavya said coolly, and once again the others burst out laughing.

'Killed it,' Aakash hooted.

'She's emasculating you, dude.' Mahir was literally in tears.

Even Veera was laughing. 'It's really heartening to see y'all having such a blast at my expense, you guys,' Siddharth grumbled. Veera reached out and ruffled his hair in a patronizing way. 'Aww, did baby feel bad?'

'Don't get too cocky. Mahir's here and we all know the history y'all have,' Siddharth whispered, and she shut up immediately.

Mahir pretended like he hadn't heard.

'*Anyway*, Aakash, start. You'll all see what's so great about it when he finishes the story. It's pretty cute, actually,' Veera said. Mahir guessed that she must have picked this one mostly because it would be funnier than any other story, and so it wouldn't bring the mood down.

'It was mortifying,' Aakash laughed. 'How do I do this? Do I tell you with dialogues and stuff or just narrate the story?'

'Dialogues,' everyone chorused.

'At least pretend to be interesting, Aakash.' Mahir rolled his eyes.

'Fine.' Aakash took a deep breath. 'Here we go.'

Aakash

He remembered everything about that day, which wasn't surprising since he remembered everything about Ananya anyway.

'Ground rules.' Aakash looked at all of them, so eagerly waiting for him to start. 'No interrupting.'

'What else?' Mahir asked.

'I'll tell you the rest when I come up with them,' Aakash said. 'I might get really into this story, so—Do. Not. Make. Fun.'

'Just start, you big drama queen,' Kavya said, which Aakash found extremely ironic but refrained from pointing out.

'Okay.' He inhaled again.

'Ananya and I literally spent every night together, he said. 'Not like that,' he hurried to clarify. 'Our parents worked late, and Veera had her dance classes in the evenings, so we came up with this arrangement where we ate dinner together every day, alternating between her place and mine. It worked for both of us, since she hated staying at home alone in the evenings, and I, well, who doesn't like to spend more time with the girl they like? But it was also a constant reminder that she would never like me. Heh. I chose to be with her as a friend over never being with her at all.

'I don't know why I thought Ananya was unattainable. There was nothing unapproachable or haughty about her, but there was something about her that made her feel out of reach.'

'It's funny,' Veera said, softly breaking his narration. 'She said the exact same thing. She said you were too good for her.'

Aakash swallowed the lump in his throat and decided to let Veera's interruption pass. The others weren't making fun of him yet. He continued.

'So it was just a regular Friday evening at her place. Neither of us was particularly hungry,' he started.

'Wait, what did you guys do?' Mahir asked, genuinely curious.

Aakash shrugged. 'It wasn't that big a deal. We did whatever we wanted to do. Sometimes we watched a movie or something on TV . . . sometimes I got my books over and did my homework, while she did whatever it was she did. The idea was to spend time together and we did. It was never strained or anything . . . it was pretty perfect. Now if you interrupt me one more time, I'm going to start charging a fine.' He continued with his story.

'It wasn't like our parents didn't know we hung out often, but they weren't particularly aware of the details. So I was lying on her bed, using her soft toys as a pillow, instead of the abundant pillows lying around, and completing some weekend homework. Being the supremely organized human that I am, I'd started my homework almost as soon as I got it.

'"Are you seriously painting your nails?" I asked her when I looked up. "What a girl."

'"Says the person lying on a pink bed in a pink room surrounded by soft toys." She shrugged. Her face was screwed up in concentration. Must be hard to paint your right hand with the left. I wouldn't know. "Besides, I have that family function to attend tomorrow. I want to look nice."

'I rolled my eyes and went back to my maths. I could feel Ananya stare at me. "You know, this is the part where you say, 'You always look nice.'"

'The funny thing is I actually *was* going to say that . . . but I was too much of a wimp. And because I'm *that* mature, I put on my disinterested face and said, "You always look nice."

'She stuck her tongue out. "Thanks for nothing—"

'This is really weird, saying it with dialogues and shit. Are you guys sure it's fine?' Aakash stopped.

'You remember all the details,' Veera breathed, her hand over her heart. 'What a nice guy.'

Mahir, Nikhil and Siddharth shared a similar look of indignation when Siddharth said, 'We remember details too!'

'Yeah, sure, whatever.' Veera waved dismissively. 'It's perfect, Aakash. It's like you're reading out of a book!'

'It's slightly creepy!' Siddharth grinned.

Aakash scowled. 'Ten bucks for interrupting. And no, it's not creepy. You hear it this way or don't hear it at all.'

'Oh. Veera interrupts and it's fine, but I say something and you blow up,' Siddharth grumbled. 'Continue.'

'Wait a second, is Siddharth baby jealous cause Veera is giving someone else more attention?' Aakash grinned, and if looks could kill, Aakash would have died several times over. 'Next time it's fifty bucks for interrupting.

'Okay, so when we finally decided to eat, it was around nine. I took both our plates to the living room, where she sat on the couch in front of the TV with her legs up, leaning on the armrest, flipping through the channels.

'"Are you serious? *One Tree Hill*? Why?" I groaned, and handed her the plate. She made a face but changed the show to *The Big Bang Theory*.

'"Sit carefully. If you smudge the nail polish on my feet, I'll murder you," she said, and I believed her. I sat down—carefully—putting my feet up on the coffee table. Hey, I had clean feet, and Ananya didn't care! So what's your problem?' he said defensively, when he saw a couple of raised eyebrows.

'"Just a thought," I turned to face her. "How are you planning to eat garlic naan and paneer makhni without smudging your nail polish?" Honestly, I was just teasing her. I didn't know she cared about that nail polish so much—'

'What is this story? The parents haven't even come yet,' Nikhil groaned. 'I can't believe I'm being forced to listen to stories about nail polish.' He looked at Kavya. 'This is worse than hearing about your shoes!'

'Hey! I didn't even mention shoes when we were out!' Kavya crossed her arms.

'Okay, it's even worse than what it would've been if you'd spoken about your shoes,' Nikhil rephrased.

'I'm getting rich,' Aakash nodded. 'Fifty each, guys. I've already made 110 bucks; you guys are mad.' He started laughing. 'Also, you guys told me to make it good, so shhh and listen to the details.

'When I told her that, I really *was* teasing her. But she suddenly set the plate down and stared at her hands.

'"You're right," she said.

'"I am?"

'"Don't get used to it." She rolled her eyes. "Guess I'll eat later."

'I stared at her. "Don't be stupid, it's nail polish. Just eat and put it on again."

'"PUT IT ON AGAIN?" she gasped in mock horror, and damn, she did it well! "I did not just waste an hour doing a French manicure to ruin it right away."

'"Yes, because that is so much more important than food." I started laughing. I couldn't help it.

'"I will not let hunger come in the way," she said defiantly, but I could see she was trying not to laugh.

'"Wow, priorities." I didn't see how I could convince her but I didn't want her to eat alone later, so I put my plate down. I wasn't that hungry anyway. She saw me do that but didn't say anything. We watched *The Big Bang Theory* for a while, when suddenly she spoke.

'"Feed me—"'

'WHAT!' Veera started laughing. 'I can *totally* imagine the look on your face when she said that.'

'Wow, that's damn cool, Aakash!' Mahir thumped him on the back. 'Too bad you wouldn't do it.'

'Wait a second, what makes you think I didn't?' Aakash was so indignant that he forgot about the fine.

'Please! We all know how you were. A fledgling, an innocent, poor kid. You wouldn't grow your hair, listen to English songs or watch even U/A movies! You would literally run at the name of "love" or "like",' Nikhil said incredulously.

'I wasn't that bad.'

'Yes, you were.' Siddharth nodded. 'Trust me, I know. You wouldn't have done it.'

'But she was *Ananya*,' he said forcefully, his voice breathy when he said her name.

'But she was Ananya,' Siddharth conceded. 'Anything is possible. Continue.'

'"What!" I was stunned, and confused.

'"Feed me, you idiot. Otherwise just eat your food quietly," she said.

'This was Ananya, who would throw my mind into a tizzy just by being around me. The request completely stumped me. It seemed like a supremely silly and yet intimate request.

'When I looked up at her, expecting her to be embarrassed or having second thoughts, she just stared back at me. Obviously I couldn't say no. It wasn't like I didn't want to feed her, I just didn't know . . . how. Feeding someone seemed so easy in the movies, but in real life—with Indian food, don't forget—it hardly seemed doable. So I asked her.

'"How?"

'She started laughing. Her whole face lit up when she laughed. "Just put it into my mouth, I won't bite! I could . . . but I won't."

'"Okay, let's try this." I couldn't help smiling. She scooched closer and crossed her legs—I'm assuming that the nail polish had dried.

'I tore off a piece of the naan and, after scooping some paneer with it, dropped it into her mouth.

'"That was terrible!" she laughed. "Eat your food now."

'So for the next half an hour or so, this went on. I fed her, then fed myself. It was pretty funny, actually. She moved so much that I practically had to hold her jaw straight to feed her. And my hands were shaking because she was so close. Finally she went into the bathroom and came out with a towel to drape over her clothes.

'"Now you can spill all you want, it doesn't matter," she laughed. "I know this is making you nervous."

'She had no clue about the effect she was having on me. I don't even know why, I mean she was literally the only girl in my life who could make me this jittery by fucking sitting next to me! This was all so new to me . . . but wait, I digress.

'So by the time we were halfway through, there was gravy around her mouth because clearly I wasn't very good at the feeding business. If someone saw us at that moment, it would have looked like I was forcing food down her throat.

'And that's exactly what happened. I mean, the someone-actually-walking-in-on-us bit—her parents.'

'Oh shit!' Nikhil's eyes were practically out of his sockets. 'They entered while you were feeding her?'

'Not only that, we were facing each other—our faces were this close.' He held up two fingers, a millimetre apart. 'She had a towel wrapped around her *and* I was trying to get her to eat the last bit of that stupid naan. And on TV, Penny and Leonard were kissing! *Kissing!*'

'That's what you're scandalized by?' Kavya was close to tears, she was laughing that hard. 'This is gold. Please continue.'

'"Just open your mouth."

'She shook her head stubbornly.

'"It's the last freaking piece. Just say aah."

'"Why is it such a big deal? You eat it," Ananya said. "And you haven't even finished your own food."

'"Because I was too busy feeding you." That girl could be really exasperating sometimes. "Can you please just eat it for me?"

'She pouted, and I smiled instantly. And seeing me smile (at least I hope it was because of that), she smiled. She jutted her chin forward, cueing me to hold it for support, and opened her mouth. I was just about to feed it to her when the door opened. We froze.

'"Hi . . .?" Her dad looked utterly confused.

'"Why are you blocking the doorway, go ahead—oh." Her mother came into view, shutting the door behind her. "Oh, hi!"

'That was so embarrassing. I wasn't even her boyfriend—not that that would have helped much. But I was just some friend of hers—some guy friend of hers—whom her parents were meeting for the first time. And like this.

'Thank God my brain hadn't frozen. I shoved the last piece of naan into her mouth and stood up, introducing myself.

'"Oh, so you are Aakash!" Her dad nodded, like he understood. "Were you just, um, choking my daughter?"

'"I was feeding her," I flushed.

'"Why?" His face was more amused than angry.

'"Good question, why . . ."

'"Why?" he repeated, close to laughter.

'"Her nail polish was drying." Then I realized how incredibly lame I sounded. Thankfully, her mom started laughing.

'"I guess I can appreciate that." She smiled and laid a hand on Uncle's arm. "Let's go get dinner."

'Just as they disappeared into the kitchen, I looked at Ananya in a panic.

'"You did good." She nodded, trying to keep a straight face and failing miserably. She still had some gravy on her chin. I pulled the edge of the towel wrapped around her and pushed it at her face.

'"Wipe your face."

'She did so without arguing, unable to stop smiling.

'"What's so funny?" I hissed.

'"Your face is funny," she giggled.

'"Uh-huh?" I was embarrassed as hell, but her laughter was infectious. The whole thing was damn weird.

'"Even if you *did* make a bad impression—which you didn't—why does it matter?" she asked me.

'I wish I had an answer to give her. How was I supposed to tell her that I didn't want the parents of the girl I liked to hate me?

'"Because they're your parents and I'm . . . I'm . . . your friend," I finished lamely.

'"Are you scared that they'll tell me not to meet you again?" she asked, an impish gleam in her eyes.

'I snorted. "No, of course—wait, what? They could do that? You could do that?"

'Ananya started laughing. She slung an arm around my shoulder. "Of course not, idiot. Because they won't tell me to stop seeing you."

'Her parents came back with their plates, so I couldn't answer.

'"Aunty, Uncle, goodnight. I think I should get going now."

'"But you haven't finished your food yet!" Aunty said, looking at my unfinished naan. "Come on, and Ananya, introduce us to your friend properly."

'I tried to get out of it. And really, the way Aunty said "your friend" was unnerving, like she knew something I didn't. But they didn't let me go.'

Aakash stopped the narration. 'You guys haven't interrupted me for a really long time . . . Are y'all okay?'

'JUST GO AHEAD WITH THE DAMN STORY,' Siddharth yelled, and everyone joined in.

'Okay, okay, God!

'So all through dinner, her parents were perfectly cordial and Ananya was her regular self, but I felt like I was sitting on a landmine. It wasn't just the fear of having already made a bad impression, I was also super conscious about making a bad impression now. I wanted them to like me. I didn't want them to think there was something going on between me and her. I didn't want them to not trust her with me.'

'Too melodramatic,' Nikhil coughed.

Aakash scowled but continued.

'After dinner, Ananya went to help her mom in the kitchen, promising to be back in five minutes. I was alone with her dad and I was seriously shitting my pants.

'After a silence that lasted only a few seconds, but seemed to stretch forever, during which I diligently studied their indoor plants, Uncle finally spoke.

'"So," he said, not looking at me. "Are you my daughter's future boyfriend?"'

'This cannot be happening! WHAT!' Kavya was pummelling Nikhil's arm in excitement.

'Serious shit, dude,' Siddharth whistled, shaking his head.

'Being the incredibly smooth dude that I am, I stammered an incoherent reply.

'"Whaaa—no . . . what?" I mean, imagine my shock. "No, um, I think you've misunderstood, Uncle.'

'"I'm pretty sure I haven't." He looked up at me now, smiling. "I can see it in your face. You like her."

'"But I'm not her boyfriend," I replied stupidly, not even denying his allegation.

'"I said *future* boyfriend. She likes you too," her dad said. "But she isn't exactly the type that will admit it any time soon."

'I sighed. "Really?" Yeah, I was that desperate—I actually asked her father for validation. And as an afterthought I added, "Not that I'm complaining, but you're okay with this situation . . .?"

'He snorted, "Oh no, I'm not okay with it. But there is hardly anything I can *do* about it. And Ananya was bound to start liking a boy or dating soon—I'm just relieved that she didn't pick some strange hipster boy. Better you than someone else."

'I didn't know what to say, so I just awkwardly nodded.

'"So, you do like her?" And he was smiling!

'"What gave it away? The weird food feeding or my nervousness, or the fact that I've been a complete fool tonight?" I shook my head. I couldn't believe that I was so easy to read. I also couldn't believe that I had just spoken to Ananya's father like I would to you guys.

'"A little bit of everything. There are also other things, of course. Like the time when the party went on too late and Ananya told me that you walked her to the door."

'"But everyone does that. It's basic manners," I said.

'"You weren't invited to that party."

'I flushed. Ananya had called up to talk while she walked home, and I freaked because she was walking home alone, so I'd gone to walk with her. What else was I supposed to do, right?

'"Trust me, she likes you too—and if you stay like this, I think I'll like you too." I started laughing at that.

'"So you aren't going to ban me from your house?"

'"Ananya was right! You *are* dramatic. What would I ban you for? Feeding her when her nails were wet? A bit stupid, don't you think?"

'The man had a point.

'"Thank you, Uncle." I didn't know what else to say. "And please, do not mention this to Ananya. I'm begging you!"

'"Of course not!" he laughed. "She's happy, and as long as she is, I'm fine."

'"And how do you think Aunty will react?'

'"Are you kidding? She was in love with you from the moment she walked in the door. According to her, any guy who is ready to feed a girl when her nail polish is drying is a keeper. In the kitchen she couldn't stop talking about you! I'd say you're doing fine."

'"Umm . . . Thank you." I *really* didn't know what else to say!

'After Ananya returned, she walked me to the door. "Thanks for feeding me my dinner," she grinned, and then winced. "Also, sorry you had to go through that. I didn't know they were coming home early today."

'"Thanks for not biting my finger off. And I loved them, don't worry . . . after I got over my initial panic attack, that is!"

'"Goodnight, idiot," she said, laughing, and shut the door, and yeah, then I took a boring, long walk home.'

For a minute no one spoke.

'Guys? I'm done,' Aakash clarified.

'Wow,' Siddharth said, scrunching up his face. 'That was . . . wow.'

'Are you sure this happened for real?' Mahir asked suspiciously. 'I feel like you made this up . . . made it up *really* well.'

'This only happens in movies, seriously,' Kavya said.

'I can confirm that all of these things did, in fact, occur. And they occurred exactly like he said they did. Though I didn't know about Uncle talking to you, because obviously Ananya didn't know about that,' Veera said.

'So you knew all along? You knew that she liked me, you knew that I liked her . . . and everything I did was known to you?' Aakash asked.

Veera nodded. 'Duh, dude, she *is* my best friend.' She stressed on 'is', the present tense, like she was daring anyone to correct her. No one did.

'I can't believe you remember everything—what she said, what she did . . . just everything,' Nikhil said, facing the front again and leaning back.

'Of course I remember,' Aakash almost whispered.

What he didn't say was that he could never forget. Every feature, every expression that ever flitted across her face, he had memorized. How it felt when she entwined her hand in his, the softness of her fingers, every line on her palm was etched into him. He remembered the way her brown eyes filled with tears, he knew every nervous tic of hers—the playing with her hair, the strained swallowing . . . He remembered her funny laugh, which she had said sounded like a dying whale, but which was just the happiest sound in the world for him. He remembered the time she had told him that her ultimate goal in life was to achieve the I-just-rolled-out-of-bed-and-still-look-glamorous look and that she loved wearing her hair in a bun but never did because she thought it made her look manly. He remembered itching to tell her she was beautiful to him, no matter what she did with her hair or her face or her clothes. He wanted to tell her that even if he could never see her face, he knew a million other things of hers that he could fall in love with—her voice, her laugh, her sarcasm, even her tears. But he never did.

She was proud of him and always showed it. He'd never had a friend like that. Whatever was important to him was also important to her. And there wasn't a single school competition that Aakash participated in that Ananya didn't attend, to cheer him on. He'd forgotten how to function without her. Everything was a little off balance without her.

'So why did you guys break up?' Mahir asked suddenly, and the entire van went silent.

'Firstly, you have to be dating to actually break up, and second—' Aakash started but was interrupted by sudden music blaring from the front, making everyone jump.

'Aslesha!' Kavya yelled. 'Lower the damn volume! I thought you were asleep!'

'I wasn't,' Aslesha said, lowering the volume.

'Then why were you so quiet the entire time?' Siddharth asked.

'I just . . . didn't have anything to contribute.' Her voice sounded oddly strained.

'I'm going to take a nap; we still have an hour before we reach.' Aakash kicked Mahir out of their shared seat and stretched out on the back seat. Despite the room at the back, Aakash had to fold his legs.

He closed his eyes. Even after all this time, he saw her face when he closed his eyes. It didn't torment him any more; it was comforting. When he saw her, nothing else mattered. He could feel her gentle breath, hear her ringing laughter and count the gold flecks in her espresso-brown eyes.

He fell asleep with his mind lodged in a faraway place.

Ananya.

Siddharth

The farmhouse was great.

His uncle and aunt were great.

The food was great.

The sleeping bags in the hall were great.

Mahir Shah was not great.

'You want to do *what*?' Siddharth asked. Maybe he hadn't heard right.

'I said I want to gatecrash a wedding,' Mahir said.

'And I want to go to rainbow land and sleep with a unicorn!'

Mahir wrinkled his nose. 'Seriously? I didn't peg you for that kind of guy.'

Siddharth rolled his eyes and continued, 'Did we come all the way to my farmhouse to gatecrash a wedding?'

'Oooh, did someone say "wedding"?' Kavya joined in, coming down the stairs. The girls had three rooms to themselves and the guys were sharing two. They'd kept all their stuff in their rooms but had arranged sleeping bags in the hall, so they could all be together. The real fun always began at night.

'He wants to crash a wedding,' Siddharth informed her. He knew, and so did she, that they were at the awkward stage where each of them would try to one-up the other. Immature.

'Sounds cool.'

'SEE!' Mahir yelled, jumping up. 'Come here!' He pulled her to his side, like she was on his team.

'Okay, I don't know if anyone told you, but sticking to your ex's best friend is a clichéd bitch-move,' Siddharth shot back.

'Bit rich coming from you,' she said coolly, but he thought he detected a smile.

'Veera, Aakash, Nikhil, Aslesha! Where are you guys?' he yelled, and they immediately came clattering downstairs.

'He wants to crash a wedding,' Kavya said, pointing at Mahir.

'Bad idea . . .' Aslesha shook her head, and Siddharth let out a sigh of relief. 'Let's do it!'

'WHAT!' Siddharth looked around as Aslesha moved to Mahir's side, and even Veera shrugged and walked over. 'Aakash?'

Aakash sighed. 'I promised.'

Promised?

'We have a campfire for dinner,' Siddharth tried desperately, and Nikhil took his side.

'Siddharth, we just finished having lunch,' Mahir said, smiling. 'There's plenty of time left.'

Veera walked over to Siddharth and rested an arm on his shoulder. She was only slightly shorter than him and he could smell the peppermint shampoo on her hair. 'First tell us the details. And I see why you wanted us to pack Indian!' she said.

'Yup,' Mahir grinned. 'So this friend from football camp—it's his sister's wedding. But I'm not invited. So technically, it's still gatecrashing. It's not even the actual wedding. I think it's the sangeet or something. And guys, the key to successfully crashing any event . . . is confidence!'

Siddharth sighed. They were seventeen; they should be doing this stuff. And it felt better to know that they weren't crashing a total stranger's party.

He smiled.

'How long do we have to get ready?' he asked, and the rest of them cheered.

Nikhil

When they met outside the farmhouse an hour later, Nikhil had to admit that everyone had cleaned up well. All the boys were in bright sherwanis—Mahir in emerald green, Nikhil in red, Siddharth in deep blue and Aakash in cream.

Aslesha had tied her long, straight, brown hair in a high pony and was wearing a flowing purple anarkali. And as she came down the stairs, Siddharth whistled. Nikhil laughed as Aslesha rolled her eyes.

'Veera! Come fast, we are getting late!' he said, tapping his foot impatiently.

'Coming, coming!' Veera hurried out of her room, looking beautiful as usual, in a deep-pink lehenga, a yellow blouse with a plunging back and a parrot-green dupatta. Mahir offered her his arm to help her down the stairs and Nikhil saw a flash of annoyance on Siddharth's face.

'How do I look?' a voice whispered in his ear. He turned, smiling even without realizing it.

Kavya was wearing a long gown that shimmered like liquid gold in the fading afternoon sun. Her hair was coiled into a bun, held by a single butterfly pin, little ringlets escaping down to frame her face. Her eyes were lined with a bright green that made her brown eyes appear darker and her lashes, thicker. Not that they needed to be thicker.

He had to admit, she looked pretty damn awesome.

'How do I look?' she asked a little impatiently now.

'I've seen better,' he grinned, repeating what he'd said that day, and to his surprise Kavya laughed. A genuine laugh.

'Just one thing—open your hair,' he said casually.

Kavya raised an eyebrow. 'What, you're my stylist now?'

He rolled his eyes. 'You asked.'

She grinned. 'Okay, go ahead.'

'Me? You want me to do it?' he said, slightly alarmed, but then he saw Kavya's cocky grin. 'You expect me to mess up, don't you? And then you get to scream at me.'

'What are you talking about? I just can't reach the hair pin all the way at the back,' she said innocently.

Maybe it was the adrenaline rush from the fact that they were crashing a wedding—Nikhil took a step closer. Was it his imagination or did her breath actually hitch? He reached over and pulled out the butterfly pin in one fluid motion that he was very proud of.

'If you wanted to get close to me . . . you could have just asked,' Nikhil smirked.

Kavya huffed. 'Urgh—smoothness is so not your strength.'

She tossed her hair and walked away but didn't put her hair up again. He smiled. When he turned around, he saw Mahir and Siddharth looking at him with pity.

'What?' he snapped.

'You poor kid,' Mahir said. They refused to say anything else.

'Now that everyone's done taking selfies, can we get into the van?' Siddharth asked.

They could hear the music from a mile away—the loud pounding of Bollywood numbers and young people shrieking and shouting, dancing to the music.

'I'm having second thoughts about this,' Veera said, just as they all walked up to the big gate with the huge banner: TANUJA weds MANAV.

'Just follow my lead.' Mahir winked. He marched up to the entrance and scanned the crowd. Then he picked a person, seemingly at random, and raised a hand in greeting.

'Oh my God! What are the odds?' he said, heading straight for Random Dude, as the rest of them gaped. 'I didn't know you were coming for the wedding!' He slung an arm around him and continued talking all the way in, waving to the attendants at the entrance as he passed.

'He's good,' Nikhil said, impressed.

'My turn,' Veera said, motioning for Siddharth to come with her. She went to one of the ladies struggling with two plates full of flowers.

'Do you need help with that?' she asked in true Veera fashion. The lady gratefully handed them both to Veera and took off without a second glance. Veera teetered under their weight until Siddharth grabbed one of them and they both entered together. Aslesha and Aakash followed their example and picked up the flowers.

'What do we do?' Nikhil asked, incensed that they were the last ones in.

Kavya scoffed. 'You're with me. And no one's going to stop *me*. I mean, have you *seen* me? Oh wait, you've seen better.' She fixed him with a stare.

'Good Lord! Fine!' He threw up his hands. 'You look great! But really tall, I feel less manly.'

Kavya grinned. 'And he finally admits it. Come on.' She grabbed his hand and Nikhil jumped. He wasn't used to this yet.

They walked in and, just like Kavya had said, no one stopped them.

It was an outdoor wedding. The sangeet performances were happening on a stage erected in the centre. There were a number of food and entertainment stalls all around. It was like being in a mela. The dance floor was behind the stage.

'It's a mela-themed wedding.' A passing waiter cleared things up for Nikhil. He thanked him and turned to Kavya.

'So what do you want to do?' he asked, gesturing to everything around them.

Kavya tilted her head. 'What makes you think I want to hang around with you?'

Nikhil drew back instantly. 'I just thought—'

'You thought right,' Kavya laughed. 'Of course I want to hang out with you. It's easy to get you nervous!'

'That's only you,' he mumbled, when Kavya had already turned around. It was refreshing to be around her. The same sort of brokenness, the tendency to misunderstand and be misunderstood and the ability to hold her ground made Kavya stand out for Nikhil. He loved how brazen and unafraid she was.

'Nikhil! Hurry up!' She was waving to him from a stall. *How did she get there so fast?* He jogged towards her.

The counter had numerous soft toys. There were dart boards placed in front of all the little fluffy toys. He looked up at Kavya. He had never seen her eyes gleam that bright.

'Soft toys?' he asked.

'*Shooting*,' she corrected. 'I love these kind of games.'

'Who knew delicate little Kavya Dhar was a badass,' Nikhil chuckled. 'You learn something new every day.'

'I may look delicate but I can kick your ass in six-inch heels and still look fabulous.' She ran a hand through her open hair and winked. 'Never trust a girl who can run in heels.'

He held up his hands. 'Okay, badass. Let's see you shoot.'

'You have to pay first.' Kavya looked apologetic. 'I forgot my purse at home. I'll pay you back when we get to the farmhouse.'

'So you only brought me along for the money?' Nikhil demanded.

Kavya paled. 'No, of course not . . . I just thought—'

'You thought right,' he grinned at her, taking out his wallet. 'It's so easy to get you nervous.' He winked and Kavya blinked. Then she punched him in the arm and laughed.

Kavya went first. The stall manager tried to give her instructions but she waved him off.

There was a short stool near Kavya's legs that Nikhil had no clue what to do with. The manager handed her the gun.

She lifted the gun, put one high-heeled leg on the stool and took aim.

Nikhil realized several things at once. He understood the utility of the short stool. He realized how purposeful and determined Kavya looked. He also became aware of the thigh-length slit in her dress. *How did I miss that?*

He gulped. There was no reason to panic, was there? Girls had legs. All human beings had legs. It was completely normal. He was being an idiot.

But not all human beings had legs that seemed so . . . so . . . *damn!* He had no idea if Kavya was doing this deliberately.

'Remind me,' she smirked, not taking her eyes off the dart boards, 'to teach you how to look without making it obvious that you're looking.' And then she emptied all the rounds into one poor dart board. Three-fourths of them hit bullseye.

The manager stared at her in shock. He wasn't used to people *actually* winning the prizes. He reluctantly handed over the extremely bright-red teddy bear that she chose.

'Look!' Kavya exclaimed gleefully, thrusting the bear against Nikhil. 'You guys match!'

'I am *not* holding this soft toy for the entire evening,' he said, pushing it back against her. 'We don't match, we clash . . . it's too bright.'

'Yeah, you're right.' Kavya turned and saw Siddharth and Veera coming towards them, having finally chucked the flower plates. In a second Nikhil saw Kavya's face change. It was very subtle and he couldn't tell exactly how she looked different, but it threw him off.

She held the teddy up. 'Look! Nikhil got it for me. It's cute, isn't it?'

'Technically you shot—' Nikhil started.

'Oh, but you paid for it! That's what matters,' she pressed.

'Why is it smiling so widely?' Siddharth asked. 'It's looking at me weirdly.'

'It's cute,' Veera conceded, slapping Siddharth's arm in admonition.

'Where are Aakash, Aslesha and Mahir?' Kavya asked.

'I think Aakash wanted to buy a turban or something as a souvenir to remember today by, so Aslesha went along to help him choose. And Mahir is just being Mahir—but he's doing that on the dance floor,' Siddharth said.

'What do you mean, "being Mahir"?' Nikhil asked, curious.

'Oh, the usual, flirting, eating and flirting some more,' Siddharth said. 'He's already got a fan following here.'

Aakash materialized with Aslesha, wearing a ridiculously large turban with a neon-orange plume, and looking extremely happy about it.

'I tried to explain to him that the turban he chose was a gag gift but he bought it anyway. He seems in love, no?' Aslesha sniggered, looking at a beaming Aakash.

'I feel like an ostrich,' he said, fingering the plume.

'You are an ostrich,' Siddharth grinned. 'Tall, awkward and stupid. You are practically the father of all ostriches.'

Aakash whacked him with his turban as the rest of them laughed.

'So another half an hour and we leave?' Siddharth asked. When the others nodded in agreement, they split up again.

'I want cotton candy,' Nikhil declared to no one in particular, and dragged Kavya towards the food section.

'Oh, *gola*! I love gola!' Kavya started jumping again. 'Get me one.'

'What has got into you?' Nikhil said, not exactly unhappy. 'I've never seen you this excited.'

'This is all me. Little things excite me—like shoes.' She narrowed her eyes at him teasingly.

'That's not such a bad thing,' Nikhil said as he handed her the cola-flavoured gola and tore a piece of his cotton candy. They walked a little distance and leaned against one of the empty tables, facing the dance floor.

'People tend to take you lightly if you get excited at everything,' Kavya said, her eyes on her gola. 'Look at you. People always take you seriously.'

'Fair point,' Nikhil said. 'If it makes any difference, though I doubt it will, I take you seriously. Seriously enough to take your advice.'

Kavya looked at him questioningly.

'I gave my parents a chance and took the chance they gave me,' he said simply.

Kavya placed a hand on his shoulder. 'Seriously? That's great!'

He didn't have to explain to her how big a deal it was.

'And it makes a difference, that you take me seriously,' Kavya said, looking at him finally. Her hand was still on his shoulders and he was suddenly very aware of that. He looked at her green-lined eyes, and he was close enough to see himself reflected in them. Instinctively he looked down at her lips. Her hands trailed up from his shoulder to the back of his neck, delicate yet strong. She took another step closer, and Nikhil's heart felt like it was going to explode. His lungs were working overtime and he couldn't seem to get enough oxygen in.

They were centimetres apart when Kavya's gola cup crinkled between them. The sound of crushed plastic sounded like the loudest noise in the world at that moment. They jumped apart instantly. His neck felt cold the moment her hands pulled back.

'I'm just . . . um . . . going to go dump this,' she said, pointing at her cup, her face flushed and her eyes bright.

'Oh yeah, sure,' he nodded. He prayed for his heart to calm down.

When Kavya didn't come back for some time, Nikhil went looking for her. He found her looking at a trinket stall. Something flashed in her hand but the moment she saw Nikhil, she dropped it back on to the heap.

'Ready to go?' he asked. She nodded. Her gown shimmered in the faint light of the stall. It was already late; they would have to leave now if they didn't want to be late for the campfire.

'Come on, let's go meet the others.' And she started walking down the path.

The others were already at the entrance. By the time they reached the farmhouse, they were ravenous and totally ready for the campfire.

'Okay, guys, campfire in fifteen minutes, let's change into something comfortable and meet in the living room,' Siddharth hollered, and raced up to get refreshed.

When no one was looking, Nikhil quietly slipped into Kavya's room and came out just seconds later, smiling secretively. He then went to the room he shared with Mahir to freshen up.

Kavya

As soon as Kavya came out of the bathroom, she knew it wasn't the way she had left it. There was something different.

The giant red teddy sat on her bed, smiling excessively. It was only when she went to put it near the bay window that she noticed the flash of silver near its paws.

She bent down and gasped. This was what she had been looking at in that trinket shop. There was a note as well.

She picked both up delicately and held them up against the moonlight. It was a fine silver-chain necklace with an arrow-shaped pendant. She opened the note and, as the moonlight spilled on it, she started laughing.

She laid the note carefully on her bedside table and then, picking up the necklace, hooked it around her neck and walked happily out of the room.

The note had only five words, scrawled in atrocious handwriting.

You're allowed to get excited.

Aslesha

No-lie day wasn't going that bad. It was easy if she could just avoid the truth. But didn't the fact that she was so jittery say something about the number of lies she had to hide?

This was her way of disproving what Ananya had said. Her friendships were not built on a foundation of lies. She was different with different people. If she wasn't, then how would she get everyone to like her?

She hated hearing about how perfect Ananya and Aakash were, and that's why she had kept her mouth shut the entire bus ride. And when Mahir had asked how they broke up, she'd nearly had a heart attack. She didn't think anyone knew the real reason, not even Veera.

Aslesha would take that secret with her to the grave.

Just as she was coming down the stairs, she ran into Mahir. He smiled in acknowledgement and they walked together in silence. The rest had already gathered in the backyard. Right before they walked outside, Mahir stopped her.

'You know, don't you?' he asked suddenly.

'Know what?' she asked, confused.

'What happened to him and Ananya?' Mahir asked. 'If Aakash cheated on her, I swear I'll kill that bastard.'

'No!' Aslesha started panicking. 'Of course he didn't cheat on her! That guy doesn't even cheat on a test. And yes, I know how they broke up.'

'Tell me,' Mahir said, looking steadily at her. 'When I asked Aakash he said it was not his secret to share. And I noticed that you turned the music up right when he was about to answer the question.'

'I cannot tell you.' She shook her head defiantly.

'I'm guessing it's not a simple answer and has something to do with you that you don't want everyone finding out,' Mahir said. This was no longer a light-hearted conversation. 'So the way I see it, you have two options. You can either tell me now or I'll call you out on it when we play Truth or Dare.'

'Are you blackmailing me?' she asked, gaping at him.

'Maybe I am.'

'What is this new-found love for Ananya and Aakash anyway? As if you can judge me after everything *you* have done,' Aslesha shot back. She was tired. Tired of feeling guilty, tired of knowing that she'd never gain closure with Ananya.

Mahir tensed visibly. 'If you are referring to the charity gala last year, there is nothing in my life I regret more.'

'Clearly,' Aslesha said, and she walked out, wrenching her arm from his grasp. She hoped he couldn't hear her heart pounding.

The campfire was brilliant. They ate barbecued snacks and roasted marshmallows, played antakshari and chatted for more than two hours. The moon was high in the sky and the clock had just struck ten.

'Who is ready for some T or D?' Siddharth asked. He grabbed a soft-drink bottle from the crate next to them and sat down on the grass, a few metres away from the site of the campfire. The rest of them sat down beside him in a circle.

Aslesha was trying hard to keep her food down. She could answer anybody else's question—*please let the bottle not land on Mahir.*

Siddharth spun the bottle. He got Question and Mahir got Answer.

'Truth or dare?' he grinned.

'Truth, I hate your dares,' Mahir said, smiling slightly.

'First crush?' Siddharth smirked. He already knew the answer.

Mahir winced. 'You already know the answer, you sadist. Fine, my first crush was Veera.' Siddharth nudged her visibly as she smacked her forehead.

'No hard feelings, right?' Mahir asked Veera and she looked up in surprise. It was probably the first time he had directly addressed her about their past. Veera nodded, still looking surprised.

'Continuing,' Siddharth motioned to Mahir to spin the bottle. Aslesha's heart leapt to her throat. She just had to survive this night. If the others came to know, they would hate her. And she wouldn't blame them. She hated herself for it anyway. The bottle landed on Aakash.

'Truth,' Aakash said, almost sounding bored.

'How boring,' Mahir said. 'But anyway, the sweetest thing Ananya ever did for you.'

'She liked me back,' Aakash said. 'That was pretty sweet.'

'Oh God! I'm going to puke with all this cheesiness,' Nikhil gagged. 'Ask a different question, Mahir.'

'Fine, how did you tell her you liked her?'

Aakash thought for a while. 'She actually told me first. Indirectly.'

'What?' Mahir looked stunned.

'Yeah. She gifted me a book I'd really, really wanted for a long time. The last page had a Post-it that said, '"I really hope you finish reading this book soon, otherwise you'll never find this note. Just wanted to say that you are the exact opposite of the guy I wanted, and dreamed of, but I can't bear to not have you in my life."'

'She told me about this,' Veera said. 'I remember her saying that she had done the stupidest thing in her life by telling you that she liked you in a Post-it that you might never see. I found it too hilarious to sympathize with her.'

'Then what happened?' Siddharth asked.

'I was slightly shocked and so freaking glad that I'd finished that book. But obviously I was a dimwit. I didn't understand whether she was just being nice or actually liked me. I was in school when I finished, so I got out of class immediately and pulled Ananya out of hers. I held the book up and asked her if she liked me. She basically went red and asked me go away before she died of embarrassment.' Aakash smiled at the memory.

'Why do you keep pausing? Hurry up!' Kavya said. Aslesha glanced up at her and saw the silver necklace she was wearing. It didn't look familiar.

'So I did the whole Bollywood move of pulling her close and said—' Aakash started.

'Please tell us exactly what you said,' Mahir said, leaning forward.

'Okay fine, creeps,' Aakash mumbled. 'I said, "I need you to tell me if you like me or not because you're pretty much the best thing that's ever happened to me, and I can't afford to lose that over a misunderstanding." She looked up at me in surprise—I was pretty surprised myself, that sounded so good—and then she kissed me.'

Siddharth spat his Coke out. *What?*

'I . . . did not know that,' Veera said, blinking. 'You were her first kiss.'

'Did he just say kissed? *Kissed?*' Kavya shrieked. 'Please tell me you kissed her back.'

'I've definitely been underestimating you,' Mahir said thoughtfully.

'Yes and yes. And now can we please move on? You guys are ruining the memory with all your intrusive questions.' Aakash's face was bright even in the dark.

'I can't believe he had his first kiss before I did,' Nikhil grumbled. 'Look at him!'

'What does that mean?' Aakash demanded, and everyone laughed. He spun the bottle. Mahir got Question again, and this time Aslesha had to answer. Mahir grinned but the smile didn't reach his eyes.

'Truth or dare?' he asked.

'Dare,' she answered predictably.

'I dare you to answer a question I ask you truthfully.' Mahir tilted his head.

'That's not fair!' she argued. She couldn't afford to tell the truth, especially not now, when Aakash had just finished his story about Ananya.

'Technically, that's valid . . .' Siddharth said slowly. Everyone seemed to be thinking of arguments against the loophole.

'Why did Aakash and Ananya fall apart? From what I've heard, they were on the way to being together forever,' he asked, and it was like someone had draped a heavy blanket over all of them. They went absolutely still, as if moving even an inch would shatter the peace.

'Mahir,' Aakash frowned. 'I told you—'

'Shut up, Aakash. Now is not the time to be the bigger person,' Mahir growled.

Aslesha took a deep breath. She could just lie. But Aakash knew the truth and she couldn't give in to the temptation to lie. She couldn't let Ananya be right. She wouldn't lie.

'I broke them up,' she said, breathing the words that she never thought she would say.

Silence.

No one moved or said a word. She looked down at her hands, she couldn't bear to look at their faces.

She continued. She told them how Ananya and she had once stayed up talking till early in the morning and the conversation had turned to Aakash. She told them that they had to understand that in this entire Aakash-Ananya episode, Aslesha had felt really left out—she never had anything to contribute whenever the others spoke about the two of them. She also wasn't particularly close to either of them. This was the first time Ananya had broached the subject with her and Aslesha had thought she could get closer to Aakash if she could make him listen to the way Ananya spoke about him when he wasn't there. So she'd called him and put him on speaker, hiding the phone under her blanket.

'"Initially I thought he was such a nerd, always buried under his books, boring and slightly robotic. Can you believe he didn't like music? How?" Ananya had been talking about her first impression of him. "I couldn't believe people thought I liked him. I mean, not that he's bad, but he didn't strike me as a guy who would actually like anyone, like genuinely like."

'But Aakash didn't know that it was her first impression. He thought that that was what Ananya actually thought of him—a loser, a loner.

'He cut the call before he could hear the rest of her monologue. "I'm such a bitch for thinking like that. You won't believe how he is, Aslesha. He is pretty perfect. He says what he thinks, he's intelligent and he seriously cares for me. I can be myself with him, he makes me feel wanted, like I'm the most important person in his life. I think I'm falling in love with him . . . but you can never tell him this. I can't scare him off. I can't afford to lose him."'

She looked up at Aakash. He looked so distraught that she felt her heart twist.

'I'm sorry,' she whispered into the dark.

'You never told me,' Aakash said, his voice thick. 'You never told me she said she loved me. You only told me that it had been a mistake, and that I should never have heard any of it.'

Aslesha didn't say anything. All of them knew what happened next. Aakash confronted Ananya and Ananya tried again and again to explain the situation to him. They never fought . . . Aakash just pulled away abruptly. He told her that it was better if they were just friends. He stopped hanging out with them. Aslesha knew that somewhere in his heart, he despised her for calling him that night. And Ananya never cried in front of them, ever. She was vacant and distant. She still smiled and joked, but she'd stopped opening up to anyone after that. The first few months were hell. She tried really hard to get things back to normal initially. For a long time she really did believe that she and Aakash would go back to the way they were. And maybe it was this hope that made it worse for her.

Aakash wasn't much better. Aslesha had only seen Aakash cry once, and that was when he'd told her that he just wanted to be friends with Ananya. His eyes were bloodshot and filled with tears he defiantly refused to shed.

When Aakash had confronted Ananya, he hadn't told her how he knew about the things she'd said—but it wasn't hard to figure out whose fault it was. There were only three people that night who could've heard what she'd said—Veera, Kavya and Aslesha. Veera and Kavya had been fast asleep.

She hadn't shouted or yelled at Aslesha. All she'd said was, 'I really didn't expect this from you. I thought you were better than this.' And that was the day she'd stopped trusting Aslesha. Aslesha had expected her to tell everyone, but Ananya kept her mouth shut. She had told Aslesha that it was Aslesha's guilt to bear, and if anyone heard about it, it would have to be from her mouth.

'Would you have believed me if I had told you?' Aslesha asked Aakash.

'Yes, fuck yes!' he almost screamed. 'I would've believed anything she said! If you had just told me what had happened after that—didn't that ever occur to you?' His hands were in his hair and he was pulling his roots so hard that Aslesha thought they would tear off.

'I was scared.' The minute she said it she knew how stupid she sounded.

'Scared? Scared? You single-handedly wrecked my relationship with the one girl I loved the most.' Aakash stood up. 'I never stopped having feelings for her. I just thought she was better off without me if that's how she truly felt about me. I didn't want her to be embarrassed because of me. I just wish I'd told her I loved her in time.'

His voice cracked. 'And she died believing I didn't love her.'

No one tried to stop him as he half ran and half speed-walked into the house. Aslesha buried her face in her hands.

'Oh, Aslesha,' Kavya whispered, kneeling in front of her. 'What took you so long?'

Her head snapped up. 'You knew?'

She nodded. 'We all did, except Mahir. Aakash told us the day it happened and he made us promise to never interfere in this.'

She stared at them. 'Then why . . . why did you stick with me? You knew, and you still continued being my friends?'

'Because you're better than this. Even Ananya knew that you're better than this. It disappointed us to see that it took you so long to confess but better late than never,' Veera said, wiping away a tear. 'I was really upset with you and more upset that I couldn't do anything.'

Aslesha couldn't help it; she broke down, tears flowing down her cheeks like tiny rivulets. She could barely speak.

'She—she never forgave me. I can't forgive myself,' she blubbered, covering her face.

Surprisingly gentle hands pried the hands off her face. Nikhil. He smiled at her but it was a sad smile. 'I know how it is to feel like you can never forgive yourself. Trust me, it'll happen. Maybe not today, but give it time. And if it helps, know that Ananya forgave you a long time ago. She couldn't hold grudges for nuts.'

Aslesha shook her head.

'Don't lose yourself trying to please everyone, kiddo.' Siddharth ruffled her hair. He hardly called her kiddo any more. He used to jokingly call her that when they were kids, because he was two months older than her. She felt better hearing it.

'Let's go check on Aakash,' Nikhil said, offering Kavya his hand. She took it without a word and they left together.

'You guys go too,' Aslesha said between sobs. 'I'll be fine.' She didn't have the right to any sympathy.

Veera, Siddharth and Mahir nodded and walked away.

She didn't know how long she sat there, sobbing till her throat was sore and her head felt like it would burst. The campfire had died down, and she felt a strange connection with the ashes left behind. They would soon be scattered by the wind. They wouldn't burn again.

She looked up at the sky, expecting to see stars, but there weren't many. She picked up her phone and scrolled through her screenshots until she found the one she was looking for. It was an iMessage chat with Ananya.

Ananya: Look up at the stars, see how they shine for you.

Aslesha: It's a cloudy night . . .

Ananya: Damn, I timed this wrong.

When she finally dragged herself up to her room (no one else was sleeping in their sleeping bags yet) it was well past midnight. She collapsed into bed and pulled the blanket over her like a shield. Like that could keep her thoughts out.

She heard her door creak open and, seeing the tall silhouette, she knew it was Aakash. She buried herself deeper inside the blanket, utterly spent and not ready for more guilt.

'You sleeping?' he whispered. When she didn't reply, he sighed and came in, sliding down to sit at the foot of her bed. 'Of course you aren't.'

Silence.

'This isn't entirely your fault,' he began. 'You may have started it, but I could have ended it. And I didn't. I'm as much to blame as you are.'

'You can't be serious,' she mumbled, her voice muffled by the blanket.

'I'm not saying you were right. You weren't,' he laughed bitterly. 'But I can't blame you for wrecking our relationship. I could have told her how I felt, I shouldn't have pulled away. You think I don't know how broken she was? And it was torturous to see her like that, knowing that I had caused that pain. If I wanted to, I could have straightened things out, but I didn't. I was hurt and egotistical. I took too long to tell her that it was a silly fight, that I was an idiot for shutting her out, that she mattered more than anything else. The biggest mistake I made was letting her go the way I did. Without closure.'

'Without closure,' Aslesha echoed, tasting the words in her mouth. They felt indifferent and unsympathetic.

'The point is, I forgive you,' he whispered in the dark, standing up. 'I don't know if you need it, but you have my forgiveness. It's time you forgive yourself.' And with that, he slipped out. She heard him go downstairs.

After an hour of tossing and turning, she stood up and walked down quietly to see everyone there, except Siddharth, Mahir and Veera. They smiled when she came down.

Kavya patted the sleeping bag next to her. Nikhil was on her other side and Aakash was next to Nikhil.

Aslesha slipped into the sleeping bag, and for the first time in about a year, she felt like her friends saw her for the flawed person she was—and they took her for who she was.

Siddharth

'It really makes you think, doesn't it?' Siddharth turned to Mahir. Veera had gone back to check if Aslesha was still at the campfire and the two of them were walking around the grounds. 'Anything can happen.'

Mahir nodded, deep in thought. 'Hi, I was just wondering . . . is something going on between you and Veera?'

'What? No,' Siddharth laughed. 'Why would you think that?'

Mahir stared at him and then shook his head slowly, laughing. 'You're an idiot.'

'What's new?' Siddharth rolled his eyes. 'Why did you suddenly ask?'

'Just thinking,' he said. 'I just had to make sure before I go ahead.'

'Hmm,' Siddharth was only half listening. Why was Veera taking so long? 'How come you started hanging out with us?'

Mahir seemed taken aback. 'It's just . . . karma, I guess. I feel like I neglected Ananya so much that I have to sort of atone for it by setting a lot of things straight. Starting with Aakash, and now Aslesha, and maybe even you.'

'You haven't said anything about what Aslesha told us,' Siddharth looked at Mahir. 'I thought you'd throw a fit.'

'Oh trust me, I'm pissed. It's sad that reality is rife with misunderstandings that ruin everything,' Mahir said. 'But it's hard to be angry when she's so miserable. If there is anything I've made up my mind about, it's that I'm not going hold myself back from telling people what I really feel. Speaking of, what is going on with Nikhil and Kavya?' Mahir asked suddenly. 'Do you feel bad?'

'Funnily enough, I don't. I feel bad for Nikhil, in fact. Maybe Kavya thinks I'm jealous, but when I see him, I feel pity. She's using him and he has no clue. I do hope he doesn't actually have feelings for her.' Siddharth smiled as he saw Veera approaching.

'I think she went up,' she said, wrapping her shawl closer around herself. It was almost 2 a.m. and the moon was shining brightly. The moonlight made her hair look like spun silver, and she was worrying her bottom lip slightly.

Before he could stop himself, he reached out and released her bottom lip from her teeth with his thumb. Astonishment passed over her face and he blushed faintly.

'She'll be fine,' he said, swallowing hard. He laid a light hand on her shoulder. 'Let's go back inside.'

The overwhelming urge to be with her was driving him crazy. At the wedding, he had glued himself to her all evening, dismissing any guy who even tried approaching her. Of late, school was no fun on days she was absent. He had become so used to having her in his life that it felt strange that he hadn't *always* felt this way about her.

Only when Mahir spoke did he realize that he had been staring at her.

'Just one second,' his voice quivered, and Siddharth frowned. Mahir's voice never quivered. 'I need to talk to Veera.'

'Alone?'

'No, it's better if you're there,' Mahir glanced at Siddharth briefly. 'I need all the support I can get.'

Siddharth glanced at Veera, his hand still on her shoulder, and saw her frowning. She had no idea what was going on either.

Mahir stepped closer and Siddharth stepped away, withdrawing his hand. His heart was thudding unnaturally hard.

'Veera,' Mahir said, taking one of her cold hands into his own. Her hand was rigid and unmoving in his, but she made no move to withdraw it.

'Mahir.' Siddharth wanted him to drop her hand immediately. 'What—' Mahir silenced him with a look.

'I promised that I would tell people what they mean to me. It might be a little too late, but here it is. I know we have a history, a sad one. We ended rather abruptly. I was an ass about it, but we're older now, and I like to believe we're smarter.' He paused and smiled before continuing. 'I'm willing to try again if you want to. A fresh start.' He looked her dead in the eye. 'Veera, will you go out with me again?'

It was as if someone had hit Siddharth with a drum. His ears were ringing, his brain unable to process what was happening. White-hot anger rose up in him like a snake and he wanted to strangle Mahir Shah. But it was Siddharth who had always pushed Mahir and Veera together, so why was he mad? Of course he was mad! After all these years, he couldn't just fucking waltz in and take Veera—his Veera— away. *What the hell!*

'What?' Siddharth and Veera chorused, equally shocked. Siddharth searched Veera's face for something, anything. She was looking at Mahir holding her hand like she had got everything she had ever wanted and lost everything she'd ever had at the same time.

'I . . . I . . .' she stammered, and then she looked at Siddharth. She took a deep breath. He couldn't figure out why she was looking at him like that. Like he was her one anchor to the world. He had to get out of here. Too many emotions were coursing through him and he couldn't think straight. He didn't want to think. And he most definitely didn't want to be witnessing Veera and Mahir's reunion.

'I . . . I need some air.' He saw Veera's face crumble as he dashed away.

He never looked back. As he burst in through the door, Aakash, Nikhil, Kavya and Aslesha looked up at him.

'Hey, where's Veera?' Kavya asked, not unkindly.

'With Mahir,' he spat, and then raced up the stairs to the terrace. He lay down flat on the ground, staring up at the sky. Dammit, even the stars refused to shine for him.

He lay there for a long time, not really thinking about anything. He shut his eyes.

Even with his eyes closed, he was instantly aware of her presence in the balcony below. Maybe it was the way her bare feet sounded on the cold tiles. He heard Mahir's voice and instantly stiffened.

'So no hard feelings, right?' he heard Mahir say, and Veera laughed. His chest tightened. He didn't want to know.

'No hard feelings,' Veera reaffirmed. 'Goodnight, Mahir.'

'He's up there, by the way,' Mahir said in a not-so-subtle whisper. Veera laughed again and he heard the balcony door shut. Soon enough, he heard her climb up the ladder. He opened his eyes just as she pulled herself lightly on to the terrace. There was no teasing, no humour or laughter in her tone when she spoke.

'Siddharth,' she said. He closed his eyes again. 'Siddharth, look at me.'

He turned to look at her, trying to suppress the roiling tide of emotions that probably showed in his eyes.

'I said no.'

It was as if someone had dumped ice-cold water over his head. Relief—more than he would have liked to admit—rolled over him in such huge waves that he felt light-headed, almost nauseous. He realized that she was within touching distance and was searching his face for his reaction.

'Why would you think I care?' His voice was raspy and that ended up sounding way harsher than he'd intended it to. Hurt flashed across Veera's face. And just then his phone rang.

'Hello,' he said grumpily.

'Hey, asshole.' It was Mahir. 'Are you still being the bitch you were some time back? "I'm not into Veera", "I don't really care what happens",' he said, mimicking Siddharth ridiculously.

'I never said that,' Siddharth growled.

'Please tell me you figured it out,' Mahir sighed. 'You said she was available, you said you didn't have any feelings for her. So I asked her out to get you to finally acknowledge whatever shit you're feeling. Technically I never broke the bro code. You said you weren't into her. It hurt, didn't it? Knowing you could lose her in a split second to somebody else?'

'So you didn't actually—'

'Ask her out? No, I didn't,' Mahir said. 'And even she knows that, so stop sounding like an idiot.'

'Jerk!' Siddharth rubbed his forehead. 'Why are you doing this?'

'I'm trying to set my karma right,' Mahir said. 'I swear to God, I hope you realize how lucky you are.' The line went dead.

'That was, um, Mahir,' he said, pointing to his phone lamely. Veera still looked hurt.

'You know what, you're right,' she said softly, not looking at him. 'Why would you care? I'm an idiot. I'm just going to, um, go now.' She spun around, but Siddharth caught her wrist without even looking at her.

'Veera—' Something in the way he said her name made her pause. He pulled her down beside him.

Without realizing it, he ran a finger along her sharp jaw and heard a sharp intake of breath. He wanted to commit to memory every expression on that face. He wanted to spend all his time with her.

'I *hated* it,' he said. 'You have no idea how much. I wanted to punch Mahir in the face for asking you out.'

'Why?' Her voice was barely a whisper.

'I don't know.' He took her hand, pressing their palms flat together. 'I don't want someone else to hold your hand. I don't want you to dress up for someone else. I want your smiles all to myself. You probably think I'm crazy, but when I said I didn't care, that's the biggest lie I've ever told.'

She didn't say anything, just entwined their fingers together.

'Why did you say no?' Siddharth asked softly. 'Before you knew that it was just a set-up, why did you say no? You've always wanted this.'

'I've wanted *this*,' she agreed, not looking at him.

'Come with me to the charity gala,' he said suddenly, and she looked up at him.

'Are you asking me to the biggest social event of the year?' Siddharth nodded. 'Will you?'

'Obviously,' she said, hitting his arm lightly. After a few minutes of silence, Siddharth spoke again.

'Veera,' he tried in vain to calm his breathing, 'I don't know what's happening.' His voice shook. 'It terrifies me.' He pulled her closer, grumbling as she laughed.

She unwrapped her shawl and threw it over the both of them. 'Do you want it to stop?' she asked. His thumb was tracing patterns on her hand but she didn't seem to mind.

'Hell no.'

That seemed to be the right answer—for she stretched and leaned against him, placing her head on his shoulder. As she turned to look at him, he wrapped his arm around her shoulder and pulled her closer, holding her tight. She smiled, and he sighed, content, as she closed her eyes.

'Then,' Siddharth felt his breath catch as he felt her lips against his neck, 'just let it happen.'

Mahir

His nose was pressed against the window as he looked out and thought about nothing in particular. Everyone was asleep, catching up on lost sleep and preparing for the hectic days, ahead. Mahir felt exhausted too, but couldn't sleep like the rest.

He couldn't believe that when they went to school tomorrow, they would officially be in Class XII. In a few days, was the annual charity gala, and the very next day was Veera's dance programme. He'd heard that Nikhil and Kavya were going to the gala together, as were Veera and Siddharth. Aslesha had decided not to attend. Mahir was seriously considering asking Aakash to go with him.

Almost as soon as he was dropped off home, Mahir dumped all his stuff in his room, grabbed the cream-coloured envelope and rushed out again.

After Ananya's death, Mahir had unconsciously started spending more time with her group. And now, months later, he was closer to them than anyone else in his school. For a while, Mahir's 'group' had left him alone. After that display in the assembly, Sunayana and the likes of her had backed off. But he could feel the social pressure building again. He was constantly added to WhatsApp groups for wild plans, girls had started Snapchatting him again, and he was getting invited to random parties. He didn't want all that. He just wanted to spend his senior year in peace with the people he considered friends. And he was afraid that once school started, he would be sucked back into the race for popularity.

He wandered into a Starbucks, bought himself an espresso macchiato and settled down at a table overlooking the street. Ananya always said that she judged the strength of a person's character by how they take their coffee. *You either drink coffee strong or not at all.*

He slipped the sheaf of papers out of the envelope and stared at it for a minute. He was already pretty sure what this letter would be about. This time last year, they had all been at the charity gala. Mahir and Ananya had gone together in a rare show of friendship. She had begged and pleaded that he shouldn't enter with her because, *duh,* Mahir Shah shouldn't be seen with Ananya Krishnan. Mahir had told her not to be silly and promised to be with her the entire time. But almost from the minute they walked in, he'd been sidetracked. Ananya didn't seem to mind, she was hanging out with her group. Mahir was dating Sunayana at the time, and she had been incensed that he had brought another girl to the gala. When they were dancing, she had pushed Ananya away in front of everyone, asked her how she thought she was worthy of being brought to the gala by the most popular boy in school and started dancing with Mahir like nothing had happened. And Mahir had gone along with it.

Siddharth had been mad at him for a month after that. Ananya obviously hadn't taken it lying down, but that didn't stop her from feeling humiliated. When Mahir had asked Siddharth why he never shouted at him for his behaviour that day, Siddharth had shaken his head and said that Ananya had made him promise not to say a word to him.

Mahir,

I'm not in love with you.

I would be lying if I said that I had never contemplated being in love with you. But I know I'm not. I'm in love with the idea of you. And it's not good for me. I'm in love with all that you can be if you chose to. I'm in love with the sensitivity inside you. I'm in love with the concept of the Bad Boy who was good only to his Good Girl.

I'm not sure you understand why today was such a big deal for me. You know when you've based your life on just ONE belief and then you wake up one day and realize that maybe you were wrong all along? That's how I feel.

I based my life around you. You were my grand success. A proof that second (or third, fourth, fifth, whatever) chances were worth giving. That a person is never beyond changing. We went months without talking, but somehow you always came back to me. It could be a text at two in the morning, or a random phone call in the middle of the day—the point is you kept me in your life and I kept you in mine.

I believed in you, believed that the friendship that we had would bring you to my immediate defence when I needed you, if I ever did. And when you could've stepped up, you didn't. This will never visibly change anything between us because I will never be able to tell you this to your face. But maybe, just maybe, I was wrong in believing that you would do for me what I would do for you.

I'll always be there for you when you need me, but I will never again put myself in a situation where I'll need you.

I need you to understand that you have to start doing what you want. Set things straight. Don't put popularity above everything that matters to you. If nothing else, don't be fake. I like to believe that the guy you are when you're with me is the real you—the guy who laughs a little freer, talks about his passions and ambitions with fierce love and doesn't filter his thoughts before sharing them. The guy who used to once consider relationships sacred.

You know what I love about you? You always try. When you get into anything, be it a class or even a relationship, you give it your all. But you cannot continue to self-destruct to atone for the hearts that you think you've broken.

I don't know about you, but I'll always have a soft spot for you. Why, I don't know. Maybe because your influence, in some ways, has made me who I am today or maybe because there are bound to be remnants of the huge emotional investment I made in you.

One way or another, Mahir, you have to start making decisions. Life is short, so just live it the way you want to and with the people you want to spend it with. Being fake happy is honestly worse than being sad.

Just one last thing.

If you knew you wouldn't fail, what is the first thing you would do? Now go out and do it.

Because despite everything, I still believe in you.

Ananya

When he looked up from the letter, his mind took a second to process it. In a way, the letter was exactly what he had expected, and then again, it wasn't. He had expected accusation after accusation condemning him to the depths of hell, but what he'd got instead was a slightly sad letter about how she still cared about him after everything.

He scanned the crowd in the café to see if he recognized anyone and swore when he spotted Niharika with her clique. Just then the door opened and Kavya walked in with Nikhil.

Oh great. This would be awkward. Who was he supposed to spend time with? Would Niharika have an issue if he sat with Kavya and Nikhil and not her? Would she expect him to flirt with her like he used to?

Niharika spotted them before they spotted Mahir.

'Baby, hi!' Niharika got up, swaying unsteadily for a minute in her tall heels, and pulled Kavya into a hug. None of them had seen Mahir yet. Maybe he could just quietly slink away. He slid out of his seat slowly.

Kavya's face was stony. She let herself get pulled into a hug. Mahir turned to go.

'No, you know what?' a voice rang loudly. 'Fuck you, Niharika.' He stopped dead. He turned around and stared at the girls. Niharika, too, wore an expression similar to Mahir's. With a shock he saw that it was Kavya who'd spoken.

Um . . . *plot twist?*

He knew that Niharika and Kavya weren't the best of friends, but they always pretended to be!

'You have *always* got on my nerves. Always! When I was with Siddharth, you constantly hit on him—shamelessly. You spread stupid rumours about me like an immature little idiot. You'd give plastic a run for its money with that attitude of yours. I don't know if anyone ever told you, but being fake is not the new trend. You have *no* idea how long I've been wanting to tell you this,' she continued, while Nikhil was looking at her like he couldn't be more proud.

'So you, your stupid minions and that ridiculous outfit you're wearing can go to hell for all I care.' She turned to Nikhil. 'I don't feel like coffee any more. Let's go.'

Mahir looked around, alarmed. People were starting to stare. He saw Nikhil's face and wondered if he had something to do with this change in Kavya.

Niharika's face looked red enough to burst. She looked around wildly and, in a stroke of extreme bad luck, she saw Mahir. Mahir almost laughed at the mess he was in.

'Mahir!' she shrieked.

'Hiii, guys!' Mahir nodded awkwardly. 'What are the odds I'd meet you all here, huh!'

Kavya and Nikhil turned to see Mahir. 'Oh hi, Mahir,' Nikhil grinned widely, loving the drama.

'You *talk* to these losers? Since when?' Niharika shrieked. He was really getting tired of that noise.

'Since he realized you were too tacky to be seen with,' Kavya said with an Oscar-worthy eye-roll.

Okay, not good, Mahir thought to himself. *If I go against her now, senior year is going to be so, so awkward.* He cringed.

I still believe in you.

Ananya.

'Since the time I realized that you are nothing but a fake-ass lowlife who makes everybody's life her business because she's so clearly unhappy with her own.' He stepped into the spot beside Kavya.

'MAHIR!' Niharika (predictably) shrieked. 'You watch. I will make your last year at school hell. No one will speak to you. You do not want to cross me!'

'These people,' he gestured towards Nikhil and Kavya, 'are twice the friends you or your gang will ever be, not to mention that outfit really is ridiculous. Why would you willingly wear that in public?'

'Maybe you aren't a complete asshole, after all,' Kavya laughed, as Niharika stomped her feet and made a perfect diva exit.

Mahir waved goodbye as she opened the door. It was liberating. He should have done this way back.

'You know,' Niharika paused on the way out, trying desperately to have the last word, 'swearing is unattractive!'

'Well then,' Kavya said, smirking, 'fuck you.'

Kavya

Today was the charity gala. Kavya had had her dress picked out long ago. She had really been looking forward to it.

She smoothed her dress down self-consciously. She was wearing a blood-red sheath dress with a sweetheart neckline and a plunging back. Her hair was in a high ponytail and the silver-arrow pendant rested on her collarbone. Suddenly she reached up and pulled off the rubber band holding her hair, letting it tumble around her face in cascading waves. She smiled.

It had been almost a week, and Kavya still couldn't believe what had happened at Starbucks. She had no idea how she had worked up the courage to do what she had done. Again, Nikhil's influence. He'd looked so proud, so happy—she wanted to see that look again and she wanted to be the one who brought that smile to his face.

She glanced at the clock—Nikhil would be here any minute. She felt her stomach flutter at that. He was another dilemma. He could never know that Kavya had initially clung to him to make Siddharth jealous. If he ever found out, he would lose all the respect he had for her.

Kavya grabbed her nude heels, her purse and Ananya's letter and went into the hall. Her parents were already at the gala and she had the house to herself. Dropping on to the couch, she took a deep breath.

Kavya and Ananya had had a straightforward relationship. They fought often but never gave up on each other. Kavya had known Ananya for a long time, almost as long as Siddharth had known Ananya, and through their time together, Ananya had always been frank with her. Between them, they didn't sugar-coat anything. That's why Kavya was pretty sure that if there was something Ananya had wanted to tell her, she would get straight to the point in the letter. She opened it and began reading.

Kavya,
Just remember that I love you despite all the things I'm about to tell you (lol, sorry).
You are stubborn as hell. You want people to constantly fight for you, but you will never fight for them. You try and convince yourself that you have no feelings, that you are doomed to be stone-cold for all eternity. You end up always going along with what people say because you are too afraid of what people will think of you. It's what took you so long to end things with Siddharth.
You had a huge fight with him the other day and almost broke up with him. But you didn't. And the next day you were back to normal because—what would people think, right?

Can I honestly tell you why we all wanted you and Siddharth to stay together? Initially, yeah, you guys were really into each other. But with time that faded, and that was no one's fault. Both of you dragged it on till it became too bitter. And we're all to blame—we encouraged you to drag it on forever. Why? Because it made things easy. For us.

Siddharth being with you meant that somehow all of us would always be involved in his life and he would always be involved in ours. He would have to split his time between all his friends. I know, it was incredibly selfish, but it's the truth. You wondered why everyone blamed you for the break-up, this is the reason.

You have absolutely no idea how much I respect you for the way you held yourself during those months. You didn't break down, you didn't ask for our support (which was good because we weren't very sympathetic at the time) and you showed everyone that a girl doesn't need a guy, to be taken seriously.

But you know what I'm scared of? I'm scared that every time someone shows you how they feel, you won't accept it. You are so busy thinking of all the reasons things could go wrong that you never see what would happen if they worked. And wow, you really are the *queen of procrastination. You procrastinate feeling your feelings. But K, how long can you really hide from yourself?*

Do yourself a favour and listen to yourself. Because under that cold, hard exterior is a soul that is begging for acceptance.

Love,
Ananya

It was liberating to think that the break-up wasn't completely her fault. She remembered the day Ananya was talking about perfectly well. Siddharth had accused her, none too subtly, of cheating on him and she had lost it. It was beyond humiliating and, for the first time in God knows how many years, Kavya had cried herself hoarse in the bathroom, folding herself into Ananya, who held her without protest. Through her tears she had sworn again and again that she didn't want to be with Siddharth any more, that she was tired of trying. And yet, Ananya was right, the next day Kavya was back with him, smiling like nothing had happened. A month later, they had broken-up. If she had one regret, it was that she waited too long. She wished that she had broken up with him before he had.

The doorbell rang and she quickly stuffed the letter into her purse, slipped her heels on and opened the door.

Nikhil stood outside in a tuxedo, looking incredibly good, and Kavya's heart fluttered. She would not lose him.

He gave her a once-over. 'Not bad, Dhar. You look amazing.'

'You're not too bad yourself,' Kavya grinned. 'Ready to go?'

The charity gala was the grandest event Agastya International hosted. It invited all the social and political bigwigs of Mumbai to make donations to various NGOs. It was an annual event the school was proud of. They had the most expensive and delicious food for the occasion. The auditorium and the grounds were tastefully decorated in cream silk and Kavya's red dress stood out beautifully.

It had been a while since they'd reached, but they hadn't seen any of their friends yet. Nikhil had persuaded Kavya to dance with him. She had refused initially but he'd asked so cutely, she couldn't say no. So after a little dancing, eating and socializing, here she was, sipping her drink and surveying the crowd. There were a lot of people she knew, but strangely, she couldn't be bothered to make small talk with anyone. Nikhil had just gone to get himself something to eat.

'Is that champagne?' a voice asked from behind, and Kavya smiled.

'Hey, Veera,' she said, and inclined her head in Siddharth's direction. 'And Siddharth. And no, it's Appy Fizz in a flute. It seems a much classier way to drink it!'

Veera looked radiant in her emerald-green asymmetrical dress. Kavya didn't think someone could actually *glow* with happiness, but Veera really was.

Siddharth lightly touched Veera's back to get her attention. 'I'm just going to get a glass of water. You guys want anything?' he asked, looking at Kavya. 'And where is Nikhil?'

'Oh, I think he went to get something to eat. If you find him, bring him back with you, please,' she said, nodding towards the buffet. Siddharth grinned and walked away.

'I have been meaning to talk to you,' Veera said, suddenly fidgeting with her nails.

Kavya sighed. 'Me too. I know things haven't really been that great between us and I guess that's basically my fault. I'm sorry.'

Veera blinked. 'I'm sorry too. But that's actually not what I wanted to talk to you about.'

'Really? Then spill.' Kavya took a sip of her drink.

'I want your permission.'

'For what?' Kavya laughed. Since when did Veera need her permission? 'Veera, you're freaking me out.'

Veera took a deep breath. 'You can still have Siddharth back, Kavya.'

Kavya narrowed her eyes. 'What do you mean?'

'I mean, if you still like him and don't want him to be with another girl, I'll back off.' She looked up at Kavya with her big brown eyes. 'I mean it.'

'What do you want from me, V?' Kavya asked.

'I guess I'm saying that I don't want things to be weird between us forever because of him. It would practically be breaking every girl code in the book—me teaming up with your ex.' Veera had the grace to look apologetic. 'So yes, I want to know if you are okay with me hanging out with him.'

Kavya thought for a minute. Wasn't this what she'd wanted? Wasn't this what she'd gone through all the trouble for? To make Siddharth hurt a little? The way he had hurt her. She knew Veera would actually back off if Kavya asked her to. Nothing needed to change.

Except, everything already had.

She thought about Nikhil. He accepted her for who she was, with all of her flaws. He didn't want her to change. She genuinely enjoyed his company. After all this time, did she really want Siddharth back, just to have her revenge? She didn't know if she and Nikhil had a future or if her feelings were one-sided, but she was willing to take a chance on him that she would never be willing to take with Siddharth.

'Do you like him?' Kavya asked her.

'I don't know . . . I might . . . I just don't know if I'll ever do anything about it. I do want to be with him, but without pissing you off.'

'No,' she said, smiling. 'No, he's all yours.'

Veera looked taken aback, like that wasn't what she'd expected Kavya to say. She set her glass on the table and pulled Veera into a hug, and Veera hugged her right back.

'Touching scene,' Siddharth said, coming up from behind.

Kavya pulled back. 'You, Siddharth Ahuja, were a *terrible* boyfriend, but that's probably because our relationship itself was horrible. I've finally let you go. No more snide comments and bitterness. But you'd better not mess up what you have now.' She smiled at him and he smiled back, a silent understanding passing between them. 'Have you seen Nikhil?

233

I really have to talk to him.' She craned her neck, trying to look over Siddharth's shoulder.

Siddharth shook his head. 'Speaking of Nikhil, I can't believe you actually used him to make me jealous. You were so bad at it. What, did you start liking him or something? And for the record, it didn't work at all!'

Kavya was about to retort, when she heard a sharp intake of breath next to her. She whirled to see who it was, already praying that it wasn't who she thought it was.

'Is it true?' Nikhil looked at her, his glance accusatory. 'Did you really do that?'

'Oh shit,' Siddharth muttered and Veera pulled him away.

'Nikhil,' Kavya's voice was soft, 'it—'

'Did you or did you not?' he demanded, his voice still dangerously steady.

Kavya said nothing. She looked down at the floor.

'So it's true,' he laughed bitterly. 'So all this . . . this *affection* for me was just a plan? Did you even care about what I said, or did you go along with me just for the heck of it?' He shook his head. 'I should've known.'

'Let me explain,' Kavya said, desperately reaching for him. But he shrugged away from her. 'It wasn't a plan, it never was!'

'And you know the worst part? I was coming here to tell you . . . to tell you—' He swore when his voice cracked.

'To tell me what?' Kavya said, holding her breath.

'It really doesn't matter, does it?' he looked at her, broken. 'I opened up to you and you exploited me. I thought I knew you.' He turned on his heel and walked away, away from her.

She wanted to cry but the tears wouldn't come. She didn't know what to do. She would have stood there and watched him walk away if Ananya's words hadn't come back to her.

You want people to constantly fight for you but you will never fight for them.

She was not going to let him go.

She removed her heels and ran after him.

She found him brooding in the grounds, sitting on a wooden bench. His head was in his hands and he looked distraught. Kavya's stomach twisted, knowing she was responsible for this.

'Kavya, just go,' he said, not looking up. 'It's fine, whatever. I'm mad at myself that I let this happen. Just go. I can't look at you right now.'

Kavya swallowed her tears. 'Then don't,' she said, walking up to him. She sat down next to him on the bench and pressed her hands together. 'I'm not leaving till I make you understand how important you are to me.'

Nikhil snorted.

'I had this thought when Siddharth saw us together at Carter's, and I thought it would be harmless, just something to irritate Siddharth with,' Kavya started, her voice shaking slightly. 'It was stupid, immature and an absolute failure. And it was so very wrong.

'But you have to know, everything I've ever done, anything I've ever said to you is the complete truth. Even when

I was trying to make Siddharth jealous, it was only half-hearted because I didn't really even want to be with him. You saw me in a way that I hadn't seen myself in in a long time and I *wanted* to be a better person for you.' He looked up at her now, his eyes still wary.

'Whether it's two in the morning or two in the afternoon, I want to talk to you all the time. I want to fight and argue with you, and then make up. Whenever something happens, you're the first person I want to share it with. I can be myself around you. For the first time in *ages* I'm happy. And it's all because of you. I mean, look at me!' she gestured at herself. 'I'm the same person, but I'm so much better. And when I decided to make Siddharth jealous, I had no idea that I would end up—dammit!' She pressed her hands to her eyes to force the tears back.

Gentle hands pried her hands from her face. 'That you would end up what?' Nikhil asked, looking unflinchingly into her eyes.

'That I would end up falling for you,' she whispered, looking down. He was still holding her hands and a few tears fell on them. 'And the idea of losing you terrifies me. I want you in my life, Nikhil. And now I've made you hate me.' She sniffled pathetically.

'Kavya,' Nikhil's voice was gentle, 'look at me.' So she looked. And her heart leapt when she saw he was smiling.

'I don't hate you. I *can't* hate you. It's freaking impossible. You infuriate me, you drive me crazy with your antics. And the best part is you have no clue about the effect you have on me. It also doesn't help that you are extraordinarily beautiful, and you should know that I lied every time I said that I've seen better. I can't see you cry—it makes me want to punch whoever made you cry, and I've never felt like punching myself more.' He wiped her tears away with his thumb and pulled her closer. 'All I've wanted to do ever since that wedding is kiss you . . .'

And he did. It was soft and lingering, and tasted like tears and iced tea. His hands went to the back of her neck, his fingers tangling her hair, and he tilted his head, deepening the kiss. Her heart was pounding so hard she couldn't breathe. Fireworks exploded behind her eyelids as he gently nipped her bottom lip. She felt him smile. He was kissing her like his life depended on it, and yet so gently, like he was afraid she might break. And she was clutching his collar like she'd never let him go.

But human beings have to breathe and when they finally broke apart, Nikhil grinned. 'Now that wasn't so bad.'

Kavya couldn't hold it in any more. She threw herself at him and, burying her face in the crook of his neck, sobbed into his shirt. He held her gently, uncomplainingly, stroking her hair and whispering soothing words.

'I don't want to lose you,' she sobbed, 'because of some stupid, idiotic mistake.'

He pulled away just long enough to say, 'I really, really, really like you. And just because I was angry that feeling doesn't go away.'

'Promise?'

Nikhil laughed. 'Promise,' he whispered, kissing her forehead lightly.

'Just for the record, I really, really, really like you too.'
Kavya finally smiled.

'Yay, she smiled!' Nikhil said, laughing. Kavya started
getting up but Nikhil pulled her back.

'Don't you want to go back inside?' she asked him.

'Nope, not just yet.' He looked at Kavya happily.

Siddharth

By the time Siddharth had reached home it was still pretty early. He hung the house keys on the key-hanger near the door and strolled into his room, whistling. It had been a good day.

He shrugged off his black jacket and bent down, rummaging in his drawers for the letter. Where had he kept it? He would kick himself if he'd misplaced it.

'There you are!' He smiled at the envelope. Placing it on the dining table, he went to get himself something to drink. Every year, although the gala finished early, they would all stay out longer. But today he was back early, mostly because he had to drop Veera home. She had her dance competition tomorrow and her mother wanted her to practise and sleep early. It had been really hard to let her go.

They had left soon after Kavya and Nikhil returned. Sure, he'd assumed they would make up after he'd accidentally let slip that Kavya had used Nikhil. But then Siddharth's eyes had nearly popped out when he saw Nikhil lean over and casually kiss Kavya in front of everyone. They were finally together.

Kavya had been smiling and blushing furiously at the same time, and Siddharth couldn't help thinking that she looked happier than she had ever been with him. For the first time, he genuinely hoped she and Nikhil would last. His eyes met Nikhil's, and he'd nodded his approval at Nikhil's questioning look. He wished them the best.

Don't mess up what you have.

Kavya's words rang in his years. What exactly did he have right now? And what was that look she'd given him? Understanding, mixed with her characteristic I-told-you-so.

He picked up the letter from the dining table and settled down on his bed with a glass of Coke in one hand. It was a Saturday, and normally he would have had plans, but Veera was too busy, and he would rather stab himself in the eye than third-wheel with Kavya and Nikhil. Mahir and Aakash's friendship, too, was blossoming into a bromance, and Siddharth laughed, thinking about the unlikely pair. *The bad boy and the good boy, who would have thought?*

He briefly considered studying but immediately discarded the idea. Twelfth had just started, and there was a whole lot to study for the entire year. He might as well enjoy the free time he got. He was just about to call Aakash to catch up, but then he realized that Aakash would probably be preparing for that big elocution competition he had in a few weeks.

He could always call Veera, but he'd just dropped her off. How needy did he want to look?

Usually, before a competition, Veera was too busy freaking out, but this time she'd seemed quite calm. He assumed it was probably because this competition was something her mom had pushed her into and not something she was particularly concerned about.

'Don't get me wrong,' she had told him one day, 'I love dance. But I just want to dance, you know? I don't want to go to competitions and make something I love a tedious task.'

He placed the empty glass on his bedside table and drew the covers over himself. He still didn't understand why she hadn't called any of them to come and watch. She had, in fact, given strict instructions that she loved all of them but under no circumstances were they to come watch her performance. She didn't want them to see her in the Bharatanatyam costume—at least, that's what he thought. He really wouldn't have minded, though.

He closed his eyes and almost instantly fell asleep, still half-dressed in his gala clothes.

When he woke up, light was streaming in through the windows and the house was silent. He must have woken up early, since his parents never woke up before 9 a.m. on Sundays.

His first thought as he sat bolt upright was, *Shit, I didn't read the letter.* He groaned, running his hand through his tangled hair, and started feeling around for it. He remembered falling asleep with the letter near him and now couldn't find it. He got up and yanked the comforter off the bed.

There. The letter was lying at the edge. It looked a little worse for wear.

Glancing at the clock—it was 7 a.m., *what the hell*—he shut the door to his room and sat cross-legged at the foot of his bed. He slid the letter out and Ananya's familiar scrawl warmed him from the inside. For a second, he traced the familiar handwriting without really reading the words and then, swallowing hard, he started.

Siddharth,

Honestly, you could set the world on fire and people would still be like, 'Oh, no, no, I'm sure he did the right thing.'

How are you not a celebrity?

You are probably the closest thing I have to a brother and I never want to lose that. You used to always tell me that sometimes you don't like having so many friends because that means you are always struggling to please all of them. At any given point in time, someone or the other is definitely pissed off with you. But that comes with the territory, doesn't it?

There used to be a time when you would tell Veera things before you told them to me. In the beginning, it upset me; I thought I wasn't a good enough friend for you. I trusted you 100 per cent but you seemed to trust me only about 95 per cent. If you didn't consider me a sister, could I consider you my brother? But then I realized something which was life-altering for me. It's probably something you already know. You have always known but been too afraid to admit it.

Between the world and us, we're both each other's top priority. But between Veera, you and me, I realized that we will always be second priority to each other because for both of us—no matter what—Veera comes first. And sometimes I feel that's the reason we're so close, because we care so much about the same person.

Before I write the rest, understand that I'm not trying to make you feel guilty. Veera and I never wanted to share you. We got irritated when someone thought they knew you better than we did. But you know what, that isn't your problem. That isn't your fault. The funny thing is you don't seem to realize the reason you run around trying to please everyone, or why everyone seems to be angry with you.

History has taught us that equality is the solution to all problems, but this same equality seems to be a problem in your life. Because you treat almost everyone equally, no one in your life really feels special. And so everyone just feels like they're all contenders, trying to win your attention.

You have no idea how much I've been yelled at by Veera for giving you bhav. I mean, she is literally the only one who flat out refused to participate in the competition for your attention. She loved pretending that you weren't an important part of her life, that she didn't want your time, that she wasn't priority. And that wasn't good for her.

When you are really impressed with someone or respect someone, she always takes the effort to get to know that person because according to her, 'if Siddharth is impressed, there must be something to that person.'

I'm telling you about her for no other reason than that she seems to believe in you more than anyone else ever did. I feel like we are a chain, you know? Veera can get angry with me and I can take her drama without yelling back, because sometimes that's what she needs. But sometimes she also needs someone who can tell her to not throw a tantrum and pull herself together. You are that person for her. For me, Veera is the person who tells me to 'man up', and the rest of you bear with my drama.

I listen to you, I hear you out . . . but at the end of the day, for you (I can't believe you don't realize this) she is both, the person who will unfalteringly come to your defence and the person who will call you out when you're being an asshole.

You need her in your life as much as she needs you. And quite honestly, I can't wait for you to realize that. I'm writing it here because *if I tell this to you face-to-face, it will make you run and hide—just like you always do when you're forced to acknowledge something difficult.*

We know that everyone loves you, but whom do you love?

Love,
Ananya.

He had never missed Ananya more. He knew exactly what he would have done had she been next to him. He would've grabbed her shoulders, shaken her hard and demand to know why she would put these thoughts in his head. What pleasure did she get by asking such annoying, uncomfortable questions?

Even before he'd finished reading the entire letter, he'd known she was right. He'd known it like it was an established truth, just like he knew that two and two made four, or that the earth revolved around the sun.

Did he really want to do this? If he admitted it, there was no going back. What if it didn't work out? What if it was just another one of Ananya's fantasies where everything was right and everyone got exactly what they deserved?

Ananya thought that Siddharth needed Veera in his life as much as she needed him. Why would Siddharth need *anyone*? He had a great life, good grades, an amazing social life—up until now he hadn't really thought that he needed someone in his life so badly.

But then he remembered the white-hot anger that had washed over him that night when Mahir had asked Veera out. He remembered feeling like nothing would ever be the same, that Veera was lost to him, possibly forever. Now it felt melodramatic to have reacted that way, but he couldn't change the way he'd felt. For as long as Siddharth had known Veera, she had always been his confidante, his person, even when he was chasing after someone or the other. Veera was a given; he couldn't even imagine her not being there with him every step of the way. She was . . . home. And until that night he hadn't known how it would feel to lose someone who was pretty much everything to him. He hadn't realized how easy it was to lose her to someone else.

As far as he was concerned, he had two options. He could continue with things as they were—and they were good—but that would mean that he could lose her any time. Or he could tell her what she meant to him. Until he did that, he would always risk losing her.

He could tell her and risk losing everything that they had or he could stay right where he was and let the what-ifs eat away at him for the rest of his life.

He kissed the letter and mumbled a little thank you, feeling stupid and smart at the same time, and almost jumped out of bed.

He glanced at the clock again. 8 a.m. The programme started at 9 a.m.

He grabbed his jacket.

Everything now depended on how fast the rickshaws of Mumbai could get him to the auditorium.

He was almost at the door when he realized that he looked ghastly. He was still in yesterday's clothes, his hair was a mess and he was probably stinking. Reluctantly thinking that looking a little less desperate and a bit more put together wouldn't really hurt his chances, he went back to his room.

By the time he'd showered, run a comb half-heartedly through his wet hair and shut the door behind him after scrawling a quick note to his parents, it was already 9 a.m. Waking his parents to inform them of his plans would result in unnecessary questions, and he could really do without those right now.

He hurriedly paid the driver and, telling him to keep the change, dashed into the auditorium. 10 a.m.

He could hear classical music seeping out of the hall even as he made his way into the auditorium. The girl on the stage wasn't Veera.

After asking some people for directions, he found himself standing in front of a row of green rooms, with the names of the participants gleaming on a yellow plaque nailed to the door.

Standing in front of the door with her name, the enormity of what he was about to do finally hit Siddharth. He could still go back home and pretend like nothing had happened.

He swallowed hard. It was too late to back out now. He wouldn't be able to look at her and not tell her how much he wanted to be with her. He raised his hand and knocked.

In a second, Veera opened the door. She was dressed in her Bharatanatyam costume from head to toe. Her huge eyes looked even bigger with all the eye make-up and her lips were outlined with red. She looked like a fierce south Indian goddess.

Veera's eyes widened as she saw who had knocked. With a little cry of surprise, she banged the door shut and Siddharth smiled, thinking about Valentine's Day.

'Veera, open the door, please.' He knocked again.

She opened the door a crack.

'What are you doing here?' she stage-whispered. Then, as an afterthought, she added, 'Hi.'

'Hi,' Siddharth replied. 'I need to talk to you.'

'Can't this wait?' she asked.

'No.' Siddharth slid his foot into the opening and pushed the door open. Startled, Veera fell back as he let himself into the room and shut the door behind him.

Veera put her hands on her hips. 'Okay, talk.'

'Um . . .' Siddharth looked at the floor. Dammit. He had everything planned out, but it was like he'd forgotten English in that moment.

He took a deep breath and looked at Veera. 'You remember how you told me to just let whatever was happening happen?'

Veera flushed brightly but didn't say anything. Siddharth continued.

'I have wasted six years of my friendship "just letting it happen", and I'm not ready to continue letting time go by like that,' Siddharth said.

'Siddharth, what—' She looked at him, not understanding.

He stepped closer and took her hands in his. They were painted red for the performance.

'I can't do this any more, Veera,' he whispered, still looking at her. 'I can't be yours and still never truly be yours. I can't pretend any more that I don't want to be with you.'

He heard her inhale sharply.

'Because I do. I need you in my life more than I've ever needed anyone. I'm sorry. I'm sorry I took so long to realize this. But if you think about it, you've always been with me or there for me at every important moment in my life. And I can't help thinking that maybe it was you that made those moments important.

'I know we're young—and I'm having trouble putting my thoughts into words because I'm so afraid of scaring you off— but there isn't even one point in my future that I can imagine without you. I imagine graduating with you, I imagine college together, I imagine jobs together—I imagine my future with you. I guess what I'm trying to say is . . .' His voice was shaking now. He was annoyed with himself for not saying it better. 'I'm crazy about you. I really like you—I'm possibly even in love with you. All I want right now is to be with you. If you'll have me.'

Silence.

Veera gaped at him and he stared right back.

'Why?' she said finally. 'Why now?'

Siddharth laughed but it was without joy. 'You don't understand, do you? It's always been you, Veera. Since the time I can remember, *it's always been you.*' He realized he was still holding her hand and was going to drop it, when Veera clutched it tighter.

'Siddharth,' she whispered, and his stomach dropped. He already knew he wasn't going to like what she was about to say.

'It can't happen. *We* can't happen.'

Veera

They were so close she could count his eyelashes. She had forgotten how to breathe. And she could see how hurt he looked. She hoped he could see the hurt in her eyes too.

He dropped her hands and they felt cold. She wanted him so badly it hurt. But no, there were too many reasons it wouldn't work.

When he had come into her room, this was not what she had expected. And here he was, pouring his heart out to her, saying everything she'd always wanted to hear, and she had just said no.

It was always you.

She choked back a sob. 'Look at me.' She gestured at herself. 'You think I can be with you? You've always been attracted to the most interesting girls in our grade. I'm not badass or glamorous like them. I get angry superfast. I throw tantrums and I'm not always put-together. I'm not the kind of girl who will turn your world upside down. I'm not the kind—' Her voice cracked. *I'm not the kind of girl you deserve.*

'I'm comfortable and that's why you like me. I'm familiar.' She continued hating herself but she had to say this. She couldn't get her hopes up. This was not going to happen. 'But what happens when life goes back to the way it was? What happens when you finally heal and want to move on? What happens when you get *bored* of me?'

For the first time that day, Siddharth looked angry. 'Bored of you? *Bored* of you? How could you think that even for a second? I couldn't get bored of you if I *tried*. Also, I can't help noticing that you haven't said a word about how you feel about me.'

Veera wanted to tell him then. She wanted to tell him that he had been the only guy in her life. She had tried to stay in his life however possible, and Ananya had been right all along—she would go crazy without Siddharth.

But what if it didn't work? What if, despite all his assurances, his feelings faded away? Sure, he'd said that it was always her, but right now he was lonely, single and grieving. Could she trust his feelings? Could *he* trust his feelings?

It would be so easy to just say yes and fall into his arms. To stand in the circle of his embrace, to finally have him all to herself. But she also knew how easily she would fall apart if Siddharth decided he didn't need her any more.

'I can't think of what can never be,' she said, and turned away from him. She could see his reflection in the mirror in front of her.

Siddharth exhaled. When he spoke, his voice was oddly heavy.

'Is that your decision then?' he asked, and Veera had to hold herself back from rushing to him and throwing her arms around him.

She nodded, just as there was a knock on her door.

'Veera, you're up in fifteen, be ready,' the attendant's voice came through the door. Veera acknowledged her without turning around.

She watched Siddharth turn to the door.

'I don't want to lose you,' she whispered, blinking back tears.

She saw him pause, his hand on the doorknob. Then, without a word, he opened the door and walked out.

She sat for a good ten minutes with her face buried in her hands. Her head and her heart were both pounding furiously. She felt like nothing would ever be right again.

It was her turn to perform in five minutes and she really couldn't care less. Worrying about a stupid competition she wasn't interested in seemed like an insult after she had just let the one person she cared about more than anything in this world walk out that door.

She thought she had done the right thing, but if she had, then why did she feel so shattered? Doing the right thing was supposed to make you feel great, wasn't it? Wasn't telling the truth supposed to set you free?

Her heart ached for Ananya. She wanted her there so badly. She had always been terrible at taking her own advice but she knew exactly what to say to others when they needed help. Losing Ananya was like losing a part of herself, and losing Siddharth felt the same. She laughed bitterly—could she lose something that was never hers to begin with?

She took a deep breath and closed her eyes. What would Ananya say?

She could almost imagine Ananya sitting next to her, furious with Veera but at the same time understanding what she was going through.

The first thing Ananya would ask—'If you were in a vacuum and nothing you ever did affected the people around you, would you want to be with Siddharth?'

Yes. More than anything else in the world.

Ananya had once told Veera that she couldn't protect herself from getting hurt forever. But she could decide what was worth getting hurt over and what was not.

Veera had to agree that if there was one person whom she was willing to get hurt for, it was Siddharth.

I'm saying that if someone is that important to you then don't risk losing them just because they think that you don't care enough!

Veera sat bolt upright. Ananya's letter flashed through her mind, her words washing away the doubts.

She remembered the way Aakash had looked when he realized that Ananya had died thinking he didn't love her.

She remembered another question Ananya would probably ask her.

If you were to drop down dead right this instant, what would be your biggest regret?

That I didn't tell Siddharth I love him.

She didn't need any more convincing. She wanted to smack herself for being such a colossal fool.

She grabbed her phone from the countertop.

'Hello,' a voice answered before the second ring. 'Veera? Is something wrong?'

'Mahir,' she nodded to herself, 'I need you to find out something.'

She could almost feel him grinning on the other end.

'I had a feeling you'd call,' he said, smiling. 'His building— terrace. Go! Finally!'

She yelled thanks, and was just about to end the call, when he spoke again.

'And Veera,' he said, 'best of luck.'

Smiling, she cut the call and rushed out.

When she clambered clumsily on to Siddharth's terrace, he looked like he would have a heart attack. However, the first thing he asked was, 'Did you win?'

She shook her head. Her throat clogged up as soon as she saw him. What was she going to say?

'Oh,' he said. He looked like he was trying really hard to talk to her normally. 'I'm sure you must have been good, though.'

She shook her head. 'I didn't participate.'

Siddharth's eyebrows knitted together. 'Why?'

'Because this is where I have to be.' She took a deep breath. She didn't know if her lung capacity to retain oxygen had reduced, but she seemed to be taking unnecessarily deep breaths all the time these days.

'Listen, Veera,' Siddharth said, drawing closer, 'I'm sorry, I just threw everything in your face and expected you to deal with it. I shouldn't have—' Veera covered his mouth with her hand and he went still instantly.

'Shut up,' she said. 'Shut up and listen.'

This was it. She had to say it. She couldn't keep hoping her feelings would go away. She couldn't always be afraid of getting hurt. She couldn't hurt the people she loved by acting like she didn't care.

'I love you,' she breathed, and felt his breath hitch. 'Ever since we first met six years ago, you have literally been the only guy in my life.' She could feel him holding his breath, waiting for the catch.

'You have to understand,' she said, trying hard not to cry. 'I kept thinking that you made some kind of mistake. Out of everyone in this world, why the hell would you like me? I know it's stupid but I can't help it. For some godforsaken reason my mind always jumps to the worst scenarios. I become defensive without cause. It's always the 'what-ifs'. *What* if it doesn't work out? *What* if it ends badly? Urgh! It drives me crazy. And today, I almost lost the one person I care about the most.' She was gesturing wildly. Siddharth grabbed her hands and held them. He didn't say anything, which was good because if he had, then Veera would have lost her thread.

'I told you that I didn't want to be your charity case. I don't want you to feel responsible for me just because I was going through a hard time. But honestly, I have never been happier than in these few days,' she said, looking down.

'I *want* to take care of you, and I wouldn't trust anyone else in the world with you,' he said, forcing her to look up at him.

'And you trust yourself with me?' she asked, laughing slightly as he shrugged.

'I'm your best bet,' he said, and she grinned. 'Please continue.'

'When I was waiting in the green room, I couldn't help thinking about what my biggest regret would be if I was to drop dead right that second.' He smiled wryly. 'And my only regret was that I couldn't tell you how much you matter to me—how nuts I am about you. I was trying to be selfless and practical and stupid at the auditorium. But I'm selfish, and I cannot be away from you.'

'Please never try to be selfless again, it's terrifying,' Siddharth smiled. 'And do you ever listen to anything I say? There's nothing you can do that will drive me away. And you think I can stay away from you? For the past few weeks, I have literally been stuck to you like a freaking leech.'

'What I'm saying is that,' she detached her hands from his and curled them around his neck, 'I can't wait. I can't wait to be yours, Siddharth Ahuja. I can't wait for a present and future with you. And my point is, the only thing in the world I want right now is to be with you—if you'll have me.'

Siddharth looked like he might cry. He looped an arm around her waist and pulled her against him.

'I can't believe you missed your dance competition for me,' he said. 'That is so romantic.'

Veera laughed, wiping her tears. 'And so dramatic!' She had scrubbed most of her Bharatanatyam make-up off her face and removed her jewellery, but her eyes were still lined with kajal and her lips were still red. She was in her costume but her hair was free. 'Out of everything I just said and did, *that's* what you found the most romantic?'

'Undoubtedly.' His voice was low and he was staring at her with such intensity she couldn't look away.

Should she say it . . . no she shouldn't . . . it could be weird . . . oh, fuck it.

'And now that I'm standing here in my freaking Bharatanatyam costume,' she tried for indifference and failed miserably, 'the least you could do is kiss me.'

Siddharth's eyes widened for a moment and she could feel his heart hiccup. The next instant he smiled—smiled so widely that Veera was ready to make a complete fool of herself if it meant she could see that smile again.

When he lowered his lips to hers, her mind went blank. He barely touched her, just brushed them against hers once, twice . . . teasing her. She made an impatient noise at the back of her throat and, reaching up, she closed the distance between them, kissing him properly. She felt him grin as he responded with equal enthusiasm, almost lifting her off the ground. It was everything Veera had ever imagined and she couldn't get enough of it. His lips were soft against hers but also slightly chapped, and the friction felt unbelievably amazing. He tilted his head, his eyes asking for permission to deepen the kiss. He could have asked her for the moon right now. His hands were in her hair, winding it around his fingers, and she sighed against him.

'We have *got* to do that more often,' Veera said, still slightly breathless, and Siddharth started laughing. She began pulling away but he pulled her back.

'Are you kidding? You can't pull away, you're going to stick to me for the rest of your life,' he said, smiling.

'Gladly,' she said, and laid her head on his shoulders. Her heart felt like it could burst with joy.

'I love you,' Siddharth said after a moment, savouring the words. He seemed to like how they sounded.

'I love you,' he laughed and said it again.

'I love you too,' she said, looking up at his elated face.

She had her whole world standing in front of her, and he was holding her like he would never let her go.

Epilogue

Aakash pulled the curtain aside and peeked outside. The auditorium was filling up fast. It was mostly parents, relatives and friends of the participants in the audience. He could already see a number of familiar faces—Ananya's parents were there as well. He swallowed.

His eyes were drawn to the entrance as Siddharth, Veera, Kavya, Nikhil, Mahir and Aslesha entered the hall together. Mahir, that jerk—he had told Aakash that he wouldn't be able to make it! He waved to them as Siddharth found an empty row for all of them to sit. He could hear the backstage announcer tell the participants to get ready. The competition would begin soon. Just as the light dimmed, he saw Kavya slip her hand into Nikhil's. Aakash smiled to himself. Siddharth and Veera getting together, everyone had expected, but Kavya and Nikhil together was a surprise. He could tell, though, that it was going to last.

He pulled his jacket tighter around himself. He was nervous. But not because he had stage fright. His hand fidgeted with the speech in his pocket.

The competition began as it always did—with pomp and show, with the host promising that this would be a night to remember. He rolled his eyes. It was an inter-school elocution competition, not *The Hunger Games*.

He watched as the judges took their seats in front of the stage—empty but for a single mic in the centre. As usual, they introduced the judges like they were world-famous celebrities. Aakash wanted to laugh.

'Let's start with the rules for this competition. Each participant has two minutes to speak and an additional thirty seconds to wind up his monologue. The contestants will be judged on their fluency, recall, diction, expression and presentation. The decision of the judges is final and non-negotiable,' the host read out from his cue card. 'Now that we've got that out of the way, let's put our hands together for—Aahaan Talwar!'

There was a round of applause from the audience.

One of the few disadvantages of having a name that started with a double A was that Aakash was inevitably among the first three contestants in every competition. Today was no different. He was next.

The participants were given the freedom to choose the piece they wanted to present, as long as it had a moral. Aakash already knew that he wasn't going to win today. He just hoped that he would be able to finish what he wanted to say before they threw him off the stage.

By the time Aahaan was done with some pretentious story about kindness, Aakash was a mess. He never got this nervous. But he had to do this, and he couldn't mess it up.

'And now from Agastya International High, we have— Aakash Acharya!' Aakash smiled as his friends hooted and got dirty looks from all the elders present. But they continued cheering him on anyway and he loved them for that.

He wished it wasn't so terribly silent when he picked up the mic. It made him more nervous. Then, out of the blue, he remembered this lyric that Ananya used to absolutely love—'In all this silence I search for your noise.' Aakash had laughed at the time, but Ananya was so in love with it that she didn't care.

His hands were shaking so badly that he placed the mic back on the stand. He scanned the crowd and saw Kavya giving him a thumbs up. Honestly, he wasn't sure why he was about to do this. He didn't know how it would help him, he didn't know if it would make any difference. Maybe in some tiny part of his heart he hoped that Ananya would hear this from wherever she was.

All his life he had shied away from admitting things that mattered, things that could make him vulnerable. His expertise lay in avoiding awkward situations. Maybe this was his way of setting the record straight. Or maybe he just wanted everyone to know the kind of person Ananya was, and how she touched his life. It was a little too late for her to hear it from him, but he wouldn't run from things that scared him any more.

Taking a deep breath, he drew the cream paper out from his pocket and, even from the stage, he could hear his friends gasp slightly. The paper was crumpled and lined but that was probably because he had read it and reread it so many times.

He heard the sound of a mic being tapped and looked towards the wings. A stagehand was motioning to him.

'Sir, you do know that marks will be deducted for reading from a paper, right? All participants are expected to learn their piece and not come half-prepared for this prestigious competition.' The stagehand's patronizing tone pissed him off. Aakash covered his mic with his palm and said, 'Yes, I know. Now please eff off . . . I'm doing this for myself.'

He didn't wait to see the stagehand's reaction. He turned to the audience once more and started reading, determined to keep his voice steady.

'Aakash,

'You are the best thing that has ever happened to me. And nothing that happens between us is going to change that. Ever.

'When I was with you, the world was better. You made me feel like I've always wanted to feel but never could. You saw me at my worst and still fought to be with me all the same.

'You are a genuinely nice guy. And for that I hate you.

'When whatever happened, happened . . . I wanted to hate you. I wanted to hate you so badly because that would have made it so much easier to deal with everything. But I just couldn't. How do I hate someone who taught me that sometimes it's okay to make things about yourself? How could I hate someone who willingly accepted my every flaw? How could I hate someone whose name bleeds from my pen every time I sit to write?

'I've always had this fantasy that one day there will be a guy who will be completely taken by my exuberant personality, who'll think that I'm the best thing that ever happened to him. And at least for a little while, you made this fantasy come true.

'I wouldn't give up what we had for anything in the world. If I could go back in time, I would do it all over again and not change a thing.

'You broke my heart, but made sure that I didn't cut myself on the pieces. You left me feeling lonely but made sure that I was never alone.

'You have a good heart and for that I hate you, for it's harder when I can never blame you.

'When you repeat a word one too many times it stops making sense, dissolving into a rhythm of sounds that has little meaning. So why is it that no matter how many times I repeat the word love, you are the first thing that I think of? The face that is as familiar to me as my own. The eyes that looked at me like I mattered. The lips that told me I'm worth it, with words and without. The hands that held me like I'm precious. The heart that loved me like your life depended on it.

'I was so scared to tell you that I loved you because I thought I'd scare you away. But I put it down on paper because even if I'm never able to tell you this, it is immortalized (or close enough) in this letter. So here it is: I am in love with you, Aakash Acharya.

'I told Veera that we'll just have to wait and see if you are my soulmate. Because this is not the kind of feeling that fades with time.

'You are my soulmate, Aakash. Now, wouldn't it be a tragedy if I wasn't yours?

'Love,
'Ananya'

His voice broke on the last line, and for a second he couldn't look at the audience. He carefully folded the letter and, placing it in his pocket, looked up at the silent people all around. He saw Veera, tears streaming down her face, Aslesha looking like she would cry any time, Kavya and Nikhil holding hands like they were drawing strength from each other, and lastly, Siddharth and Mahir, who were looking at him with pride.

He didn't care if he was disqualified. Even if he did win (like he would, if this were a movie), he wouldn't accept the award. This was something he had done for himself and for Ananya. He really hoped she heard what he was going to say next.

'I've loved you for as long as I've known you, Ananya Krishnan,' he said, looking up at the ceiling, feeling lighter than he had felt in a long time. It felt great to finally say it.

He looked at the audience.

'And you know what? She is my soulmate,' he said, as the audience erupted in applause. 'Even in her death, she taught me to love.'

Acknowledgements

'The only impossible journey is the one you never begin.'
Anthony Robbins

Indeed, this journey would have been impossible without the support and encouragement of the greatest team of people I have ever met.

I want to start by thanking my amazing parents because you'll never find two people more constantly on my case to be the best that I can be. Thank you, Dad, for letting me make my own mistakes, and Mom, for worrying that my writing is 'too dark'. (If it were up to you, Mom, I would be writing about cats and rainbows!) It's because of you guys that I know I'm doing something right.

A huge shout-out to my brilliant friends Kirtana, Proteeti, Malvika, Meghna, Neeti, Aditya and Krish. And Kabir, who likes to show his support by gently bullying me (don't kill me)! Thanks for dealing with my drama and meltdowns 24/7. I love you guys.

I would like to thank Penguin Random House. None of this would have materialized without Hemali Sodhi's unwavering faith. I don't even know how to thank my editors Nimmy and

Purnima, who are honestly so good at what they do. Thank you for understanding Ananya's world, bringing out the best in my writing and not judging me for all the stupid grammatical errors I made.

I owe a lot to my grandparents, who never once complained when I spent days in their house, just eating food and typing on my laptop.

Class X is a stressful year for everyone, and I want to especially acknowledge the huge part that all my teachers, my principal and my fellow students played in ensuring that it went as smoothly as possible. Thank you, AVM, for teaching me to do my best in everything I ever attempt.

And lastly, I thank God Almighty for how all this worked out.

#AlwaysAnAvmite

Read More

Asmara's Summer
Andaleeb Wajid

'For a month, I'm going to live a lie.'

Smart, sassy, popular, Asmara has a secret that could absolutely destroy her street cred in college: her grandparents live on Tannery Road, a conservative, not-so-posh part of town filled with claustrophobic houses and fashion disasters.

So imagine her despair when she finds out that she has to spend her entire summer vacation there . . . possibly without Internet!

Funny, filmy and wildly entertaining, *Asmara's Summer* will send you into fits of giggles and tug at your heartstrings at the same time.

Read More

Split
Meenakshi Reddy Madhavan

Who needs love? It only leads to trouble.

Noor is having the worst year of her life. First, her mother decides to leave her father. Then, her dad's mother, the Horrible Old Crone (HOC), moves in to look after Noor (who's sixteen and doesn't need looking after, thank you very much). She just knows the HOC is going to be mean about her mother because she never wanted her son to marry a Muslim. And now Noor has to attend some children-of-divorce thing after school—and her gang canNOT find out.

THEN she meets Ishaan. He's funny and nerdy, and likes all the same things she likes. Except love is stupid, as she's told everyone, and Ishaan isn't her type anyway. He wears glasses, participates enthusiastically in the lame children-of-divorce thing, and would rather read than play football in the break like all the other boys.

Can love happen with someone who is the complete opposite of everything you've ever stood for? Can forgiveness squirm its way in with love?

Read More

Sarah: The Suppressed Anger of the Pakistani Obedient Daughter
Ayesha Tariq

It's very hard to be a good daughter

Meet Sarah. She is a seventeen-year-old girl from a conservative urban family. Sarah has to do all the chores of the house, keep her family members happy and her reputation clean so that people don't gossip about her, and always look good so that she can be the ideal candidate for the rishtas that come her way. All this really upsets Sarah, but being the Pakistani obedient daughter, Sarah can only suppress her anger. However, this time Sarah's patience has run out and she cannot hold her indignation any longer.